FRONT PAGE NEWS

FRONT PAGE NEWS

United States of America

Publisher, OSAAT Entertainment

First Edition. Fiction

Contact the Author Visit: oebooks.blogspot.com
Email: rycj@mac.com

Copyright © 2022 (RYCJ), Front page news.
Cover Design by RYCJ

Library of Congress Control Number: 2020946432

ISBN: 978-1-940994-04-8

Printed in the United States of America

DEDICATED
TO THE TRUTH.

"two sides to every story
everyone has one..."

It's true, if you're gonna commit a crime, do it alone. And if you want to keep a secret, SECRET, tell no one. It's easier to make up a story and split the loot. Besides, most people would rather be an accountant, or astronaut, or attorney, or anything but an accomplice.

That's one way of looking at secrets, when seeking quick, neat, comfortable solutions to real problems. But young people don't usually have a natural inclination to lock on to wisdom and reason in absence of hindsight, or the story about to unfold here.

These two naïve, unworldly suburbanites living just outside Philadelphia, Pennsylvania grew up in a pillowy soft community surrounded by homeowners who were veterinarians, podiatrists, botanists, school superintendents and the likes. They were educated in private schools and mentored by TV movies such as 'Buffy the Vampire Slayer', not the typical fare to walk into adulthood street savvy. Bottle fed, ingratiated only children raised by career professionals in two-parent 5-bedroom homes usually have to go elsewhere to garner real wisdom.

That's kind of what happened to Rachel and Michelle. Starting in elementary school they met, connected through a cry neither could hear, cut their fingers, traded blood and thought they would be besties for life. Like normal kids they got into trouble here and there, but had no immediate need for such stringent messages. It wasn't like they were talking about robbing banks or killing people. Warnings like that were for the really adventurous... high-rollers seeking to fast track it to Wall Street, or low-ballers venturing into petty crimes. These two cuties, though thick as thieves, began far, far from jagged crooked roads.

Most likely Rocky and Shelly could be found captured on social media; cheesing for flashes, bright eyes, calling themselves trendsetters of this and that, nothing remarkable or rememberable, posing cheek-to-cheek above familiar hashtags #lifeisgreat, #besties4life, and #booyaa among others. Booyaa, by the way, was the name of Rachel's father's 76-foot yacht he occasionally took the girls sailing on. There were pictures of those times too. Rachel with the diamond stud in her nose and Michelle showing off the big pretty dimples.

And then the levy broke. Rachel started talking about suicide after her mother, then a 56-year-old school board superintendent, slipped an $89 slender iPad in her purse. They were supposed to be out buying school supplies that afternoon. But before leaving the house her parents got into a heated argument about this shopping trip. Dad wanted mom to use the 'entertainment' credit card. But her mom hated being bossed. Plus, that card was already maxed out, nothing mom cared to explain to her dad however.

"This is my got-damn money," Ivey fumed. "I work too! I pay to be the boss," she spewed as she peeled backwards out of the driveway, Rachel in tow, using none of her mirrors or windows to check for traffic, of any sort.

Anxious and high-strung Ivey drove to Walmart, blowing red lights and rolling through stop signs, another little something that didn't get much airtime when discussing what went on in white picket fence neighborhoods. Like Ivey's exceptional history with the school board, she had history with the police department. She racked up so many moving violations that her license was suspended more than once. No one bossed Ivey, the energy she stormed into Walmart brandishing.

Most times Marcia would be working, Walmart's very own store mascot most assumed was just a store manager. She, like most of the regular employees, knew Ivey...and her anxiety issues. Of course Ivey had the money for an $89 iPad. She just didn't like to be bothered with waiting in lines, and everything associated with checking out.

But this day Joe was working, and he neither knew, nor as it turned out, liked Ivey. He, in fact, hated Ivey after she tore off his hair piece. So he cut Ivey no slack. After she ripped off his hair, he threw her down to the ground and stood in her back. This was the part that traumatized Rachel most. She would have been upset to see Buffy treated like this, but to see her mother go down this way, she'd never recover.

In short order, because the event became so public, ending up on some chick's blog which got millions of views, Ivey lost a job and a husband who also gave her the boot. Now, this initially was a matter of whose version was to be believed, Mr. Jackson's or Ivey's. Bottom line, her mom left. According to her father, he told

Ivey to get help, which she sought three states below the Bible belt, moving in with her parents who lived in Georgia. Ivey refuted this narrative. She said it wasn't true. Everyone treated her like the stuff stuck to the bottom of shoes. She expressed this many years after all came to fruition, when she was only able to get out a few words. Her memory then was completely charred, this being all she was ever able to express.

Rachel didn't understand any of what was going on with her mother. By the time Ivey was diagnosed with terminal brain cancer, her parents were in graves and her ex-husband and daughters just waking up to the realization that their mother wasn't exactly co-co puffs crazy.

This was the muse to life, and as it would be, the muse to this story, beginning with Rachel's contention over who ghosted who first. She, like her mother, would learn much too late explanations to motivations and actions, and the cancerous potential of keeping secrets...and sharing them. Ivey never shared with anyone the underlying causes of her sinus issues because the diagnosis was even a secret to her. Like who wanted to hear about stuffy noses, headaches, and I'm too sick to come in to work or be a mommy today? Ivey knuckled down, popped the aspirins and gel Nyquils, never the wiser she was experiencing the onset of brain cancer. Supermom worked through the side effects of what she decided stemmed from city pollution, pollen, changing seasons and perhaps hormonal upsets. Like most, she recognized the symptoms, just not the under-wiring that caused the symptoms. By the time her secret came to light, she was in hospice, only able to utter those few words about how she was treated.

But beleaguering over Ivey's troubles was like fussing over spilled milk. Before she ran off with a splitting headache, Rachel suffered from isolation and loneliness, and parents arguing and fighting all the time. After her mother went crazy, robbed Walmart and ran off, she was left in the hands of a father tired of raising children. He and Ivey had three girls, eight years apart...Kimberly, Kelly and Rachel. When Ivey abandoned the family it was just Rachel at home, left to navigate forks in the road on her own. That's (partly) how she ended up in the suicide lane, saved by her only friend in the world, Michelle, her ride or die who stayed by her side during those long dark walks through suburban ghettos.

The girls graduated from high-school; Rachel, with honors...and Michelle ranking #93 out of a class of 142 (on authentic documents). Printed in the commencement announcement it showed her ranking #7. Graduation night however, both girls posed for photos and pranced around as if sitting on top of the world. Rachel was accepted into the University of Pennsylvania, and Michelle was on her way to Brown. Truth be told, Rachel got into Penn ethically. She overcame a lot, worked hard and studied harder. Michelle, on the other hand, was another story.

Cut to the chase, alas the point, Michelle's mother Julia (Rachel and Michelle both agreed) was a bitch. A bonafide, hard-core B.I.O.T.C.H!

The woman first appeared on Rachel's radar, strutting around the school dressed in double-breast wool suits with skirt hemlines that fell well below the knee, and sensible shoes with sensible heels. She never had a stitch of hair out of place, and lips (always painted a neutral color) sewn tightly together. She would enter the classroom, small patent leather purse hooked over the lower half of her arm, and have a polite word with the teacher... barely moving her mouth. In fact, Rachel made a game out of watching Mrs. Perkin's mouth closely, trying to catch her lips moving. She never saw the woman's teeth, which she imagined were white as new falling snow.

Michelle hated her mother, or at least this was the perception she gave Rachel, which was not hard to disbelieve. Rachel would be so embarrassed for her bestie, who used to slide down in her chair a few inches whenever Julia made these spasmodic appearances.

That's how Michelle got into Brown. There was no doubt, though never modulated out loud, Julia broke someone's arm, or a bunch of arms getting her only child into college. Harsh to spell out, but there was no other way, dumb as Michelle naturally was, that she could get into a school that boasted a less than 10% acceptance rate. No way. No how. And anyone who fell for the worked-up essay Julia, herself, authored, and test scores she had adjudicated in small Supreme Courts, were as benighted as all the people born on the evening Michelle took her SATs at the dining room table of her family's pastor.

'Rachel still remembered 'The Wiz' school play they performed with other classmates. Michelle, happy to be selected for a speaking role, accepted the role of 'Evermean'. Well! When Julia heard this, she strutted straight back to the school, dressed in another elegant suit (she never ever wore pants) and impressed upon their teacher, who disagreed but eventually agreed, to let Michelle be 'Dorothy'! On the afternoon of the play's opening, Michelle came to school outfitted in an embellished white tulle dress, with frills and lace to go. Up against her chocolate skin, with the large white bow holding her long mane of bushy hair, she looked absolutely stunning. Everyone gasped, and then gasped again when that girl couldn't remember a single line. She just stood in front of faculty and parents, an audience of about a hundred in all, and giggled, showing off tiny little white chiclet teeth, minus one up front.

But along with Michelle's doctored transcripts, essay, test scores and whatever else took place behind closed doors, Julia paid Brown, $70,000 up front, in one check, for her daughter's acceptance letter. Michelle didn't even thank her mother. She, in fact, thanked no one. Rachel wouldn't have even known she was accepted into the prestigious school had not they been looking over their acceptance letters trying to figure out which schools fit into their besties' scheme.

"Ooo Michelle, look! You got into Brown," Rachel shrieked.

Michelle looked and shrugged. "Where's that," she asked frowning.

Interestingly enough, this was where the girls' ride or die relationship started to fray, but not because Michelle didn't deserve to go to Brown. Rachel couldn't have been happier that her bestie got into such a phenomenal school. It was, in fact, Michelle who became salty. Here she practically saved Rachel's life, rebuilding her self-esteem and courage to want to live, fighting raunchaholic classmates teasing her about her mom's predicament, all to be dumped once she was steady on her feet!

Rachel had the nerve to come up with some marshmallow plan that included visiting each other during breaks, and every other weekend as their schedules permitted. It was ridiculousness from the start to think their bestie situation would survive a long-distance travel plan, after spending every single day together for so many years.

But Michelle didn't argue. She was always sacrificing to make sure Rachel was happy, and okay, and not entertaining thoughts of taking her life. Ivey leaving her daughter the way she did was the cruelest thing she could think of, worse than all the aggravating attention Julia poured unnecessarily over her. At least she had her father, who she absolutely adored. Big Joe was her everything. Jovial. Kindhearted. Soft spoken. Encouraging. And had plenty time to put aside for her, unlike Rachel's father who had to squeeze her into his plans, taking them on Booya when he had to meet with a client… or wanted to schmooze some woman. But then big Joe suffered a fatal heart attack, in the same year Rachel essentially lost her mother, who left the family hanging. Really, they both suffered from abandonment issues, what struck Michelle hard that Rachel would even think of them splitting up, just to go to school.

At any rate, for as much as Michelle didn't want to part ways with Rachel, she couldn't wait to move out, and like Rachel, get from underneath all the things she hated about home, even if she never wanted to attend Brown. Actually, she didn't care to go to school at all. It was Julia's prodding and bending people's arms behind their backs that made this happen. That and Rachel nixing another alternative that would have nullified the entire issue.

Spelman had accepted them both, but Rachel claimed she would rather hang herself before stepping foot in the state where her mother lived. This really disappointed Michelle. She even tried to convince Rachel on ways they could avoid seeing her mother, just so the two of them could be together. Really, she didn't care if they bailed on college altogether, and ended up somewhere in Paris partying from sunset to sunup. But Rachel couldn't get there with her. "No! I don't want to be within a thought of that bat crazy woman," she huffed. "I know her. If she finds out I'm in Georgia, she'll find a way to ruin what's left of my life!"

Ms. Ivey wasn't that bad, in Michelle's opinion. She would much rather have a mother who tried to get her an $89 iPad, by any means necessary, than a mother who wouldn't buy her an iPhone under no circumstance whatsoever!

The long-distance travel discussion faded away during a summer that flew by much too quick. By fall Michelle failed to show Rachel how truly disappointed she was, and found herself on a short leash being dragged along by an overbearing mother who hustled her and two suitcases through a red wooden door belonging to

Pembroke Hall.

Right away she started pouting. The place looked like it needed a face-lift. The buildings were too old...and too big. She liked cozy, close-knit and small. Not stuffy, dark and dank. Smelled like mothballs. Looked like a museum. "But, you loved it when we came out here to visit," Julia noted.

"Yeah, but they must've only shown us the new buildings," she sulked. "Probably cleaned up before we got here...now they don't care!"

Julia made that sound she always did when her daughter was acting like a brat. She sucked her teeth and rolled her eyes. "Too late toots," Julia flipped over her shoulder. "If in a year it still looks as bad, you are free to find another school! Just make sure you can afford it!"

Michelle rolled her eyes and announced she didn't require a chaperone to her room, both parting company with barely a hug.

It didn't bother Julia however. When she laid big Joe to rest, she didn't hug a single soul. If someone leaned in for a hug, she'd thrust out that brittle arm attached to the bony wrist and pointy knuckles bearing that gorgeous 24-karat blue beget big Joe bought for their silver wedding anniversary. Everyone, except passing strangers, knew how she was. Her lack of warmth was common knowledge.

Julia strutted off, head held high and staring straight ahead, back to the hotel where she planned to stay the night, before catching an early morning flight back to Pennsylvania. And Michelle tossed her luggage on an unmade bed, before angrily marching to the campus bookstore where she fell hard for a honey-eyed blond-haired sophomore.

Joshua McKinley, the son of inherited wealth dating back several centuries (so he claimed), bumped into Michelle entering the bookstore, knocking her laptop out of her hand. But ask her, the bump seemed intentional. He was looking right at her when he walked into her. And he hit her hard too. Like a perfect aim, while she was looking right at him, with her eyes wide open, expecting a punch to the face, and maybe a few choice words that might hint at why he did what he'd done. He didn't look like a thug, but it was one warning she vividly recalled from orientation. 'The campus is secure, but open to the public and not immune from individuals who might want to take advantage of new students,' explained a student volunteer during the tour.

But the incident was almost over before it began. In a surprising plot twist, Joshua profusely apologized and immediately brought her a brand-new MAC laptop, way better than her three-day-old cute little red Toshiba. That was all it took. She hung on his every word, fawning over his mushy poetry and letting him wine and dine her in Hemenway's. Afterwards he lured her through the automatic doors of Motel 6, not the wisest he was going through Rush and on a dare to court a black female freshman for a week. If he handled his business, sleeping with the girl before midnight, he was in. If not, he'd have to endure weeks of hazing with the other brothers due to walk on line. So, he crafted that bizarre skit and went with it, a conspiracy that unraveled on week 2, when she caught her first college crush locking lips with a tall brunette bombshell. It was the dawn of her fall, completely rupturing when Julia showed up on campus.

3...

Mere weeks after meeting Joshua, Michelle made that desperate call to her mother. She wanted to come home, 'NOW!' But she couldn't just tell Julia anything. Her mother was a hard rock. Her husband passing hadn't moved her to lift a pen to send out funeral announcements to family and friends. Her sister, Aunt Lil handled that chore. So, she was hardly about to pull off her bifocals and raise up off her white chaise for any 'ole reason.

Funny, in an ironic twist, Michelle didn't call her bestie. Normally, especially for an event filled with so many juicy details, she would've consulted Rachel to use for a sounding board. But she had refrained from mentioning Joshua out of fear her BFF might think she was moving on. Before the bombshell she was just having fun, loving the gifts and attention an absolute adorable guy was giving her. He was tall, and rugged shaven, with the chiseled jawline, and sculpted abs, and hairy, but sexy legs and unequivocally most gorgeous transparent eyes. He could have told her anything and she would've complied. He was the reason prisons were built.

Yet she told her mother a man had forced his way into her room and assaulted her, and the school was doing nothing about it!

An hour later Julia was in route to Providence. As if she had a premonition she might not be returning, she purchased a one-way airline ticket and flew nonstop to Rhode Island, making dozens of calls throughout the flight. While she was not an excitable individual, privy to having fits and showing out in public, she did get stuff done. It was how and why she still lived in (and owned) the million-dollar home, since valued at a half billion dollars, purchased off a bank manager's ...and GS-14 government worker's salary. Mrs. Perkins didn't fool around.

Frustrated by the responses she was getting back from the school; deans and associate deans bumbling and stumbling through answers to basic questions, she called local authorities. She had sent her child hundreds of miles away from home, to attend a school with the highest selection process, built on hundreds of years of regal traditions, sound morals and first-class values and ethics, and not one talking head inside those pristine halls knew who Michelle Perkins was and why she was calling. Her child had described a parent's worst fear.

But the reason no one knew of Michelle, right off the bat, was because there'd been no reports of any assaults as Julia described. At the time no one fathomed Michelle made the story up, something like she'd done a few years back when she told Rachel that secret...hoping to cheer up her BFF and prevent her from thinking about suicide.

Typical Julia didn't blow a fuse. She wasn't oblivious to her child's frequent hysteria. Michelle, who she started calling Wren at birth, mesmerized by the child's coo, also reminiscent of Beethoven's sonnets, had grown up coddled. She probably missed playing her classic salon grand piano when bored, or swimming laps in the family's 16x32 foot inground pool when the weather permitted, or curling up in her warm mint colored room. None of this accounted for outright lying, but it was possible her excitable child had misinterpreted a building engineer's intentions.

By the time Julia arrived on campus a conference between deans, campus security, local detectives and the school's building managers had been arranged. The meeting was scheduled an hour after her arrival so she preemptively dropped Michelle off at the hospital. There was no visual damage, other than Michelle's disheveled appearance; albeit largely due to not bothering to bathe or groom herself. Hospital staffed promised to look after the girl, while the mother hurried back to the school for the 1PM conference.

Coolly she repeated what her daughter told her. A tall man dressed like a housekeeper entered her room with a key and forced her to kiss him. Eight blank, near identical expressions, stared back at her as if waiting for more. But there was no more.

"Look," Julia explained. "I did not send my child here to have housekeepers walking in on her while she is showering, to grope and force her to kiss them."

"We understand," replied one of the detectives, throwing up a hand to prevent anyone from speaking. "We're definitely going to get to the bottom of this because you have every right to be alarmed."

Julia left the meeting shaking hands, grateful her concerns were taken seriously, but arrived back at the hospital to find her daughter's room guarded by seemingly the entire Rhode Island police force.

"What is going on here," she hissed, just decibels below a shout.

Authorities who had been assigned to what was dubbed 'the Brown Student Case' weren't at liberty to exchange their thoughts, but in just those few hours Michelle's story spiraled around the campus and city, CCTV-cams revealed not only was she lying about the assault, but according to another student—Joshua, along with his fraternity brothers and other students, plus her dormmate, she was hardly a victim.

Joshua however, despite authority's claim they weren't at liberty to disclose details of their findings, was told he might want to contact his parents, the well-known and prominent powerhouse couple, Dan and Patty Boise. He did and they advised him to get a restraining order on Michelle immediately, part of the reason police were outside her hospital room. Of course Julia was confused. Initially she thought this massive protection was for her daughter, and was even somewhat relieved the investigation was moving at a speedy pace, but pushed pause when it became apparent police weren't there to protect her daughter, and liked to have snatched off her pearls and hurled her LouLou handbag across the nurse's station when she learned Michelle refused to be examined.

Within minutes she was snarling at her daughter, asking pointed questions. "Who is this Joshua Boise?!" And "why is he taking out a restraining order on you?!" And this one. "Are you having sex!?! Did you have consensual sex with him!?!"

Michelle denied everything. She didn't know a thing, other than everyone was lying, trying to protect a rich white kid who wanted to join a fraternity and become a part of the great American cover up protecting the likes of that rich white school. They never wanted her there to begin with. She was just a token. An easy pawn no one would miss.

Julia did that thing she always did with her teeth when her child was going over the top. She sucked them, and rolled her eyes, and eventually...after having a terse word with the school's bursa, gave Michelle what she wanted all along. They left Brown University, and Rhode Island, and returned home.

4...

A few days later Rachel called. It was time for them to make arrangements for their first visit. Michelle, of course, volunteered to come to Penn. It gave her time to rehearse a story about leaving Brown and why she hadn't mentioned Joshua during their many late-night chats, or most egregious, why she called her mother instead of her. The girls were particularly sensitive about exchanging secrets with anyone else, to include family. It was an unwritten rule that could break their bond if violated.

"So, how do you like Brown? What courses are you taking," Rachel excitedly queried, before moving on to the highlights of her first month at Penn. Unlike Michelle she loved studying and found the campus and living in the city mind blowing. She could talk for hours about the books she was required to read alone. Add on the who's who among the professors, and the many celebrities who had kids in her class, and she could go on forever. She was so far in another world talking about the hundreds of clubs there were to join and connections she was already making that she hardly noticed Michelle's distant stare. "It's possible I might get published before I even graduate," she chirped.

Michelle barely smiled. In fact, she looked sick to her stomach. She had missed her period and hadn't heard a word Rachel rambled, other than something about a best-seller book.

"Shell, are you okay," Rachel asked at one point.

Michelle had been making numerous trips to the bathroom and wasn't her normal peppy self. She loved cheesesteaks and hoagies but hadn't taken one bite of her sandwich. In fact, she barely ate at all. Actually, if Rachel had really been paying attention, she would have noticed Michelle hadn't opened her mouth since she arrived.

"Oh, I'm fine," Michelle lied, the first opportunity she had to speak. "I'm just so jealous," she said, and this was the truth. "I wished I had gotten into this school…instead of that stuffy haunted house filled with dead presidents," she sulked.

"What?" Rachel scrunched up her face. Before leaving for Brown Michelle talked a lot about partying. On one trip to the mall, she spent over a thousand dollars on accessories to match all the outfits she planned to wear hanging out, as she called it. "Well, have you met anyone," she probed. "Maybe if you hook up with someone. Did you find any clubs?"

"Girl, the entire city shuts down at midnight," Michelle huffed. "That place is like a royal pain in the ass ball!"

Rachel found that hard to believe, but wasn't about to argue the point since she hadn't been there yet. "Well, what's your roommate like? Do you like her?"

"I thought I already told you," Michelle groaned. "That chick is more boring than the city. And no," she spoke up before Rachel got back to the boy thing. "I haven't met anyone yet!"

This was really odd, though Rachel didn't air her inner suspicions. She made a face however, before abruptly switching the topic. "Well, when I come there, we're getting out," she said ignoring Michelle's horrified look. "My friend Jill lives up there. I'm going to catch a ride with her when she goes home."

"Jill," Michelle sneered with the yuck face.

Rachel caught on quick. "Oh, don't worry about her," she laughed. "She's from Kiev… some place in Ukraine…barely speaks English," she said waving a hand.

But Michelle wasn't as dismissive about the quip. It was the grease she used to free herself from the guilt of not explaining why she left Brown. It served Rachel right. She could have her little Jill, and she could keep her Brown business to herself.

The visit wrapped up quickly, and anticlimactic. Michelle claimed, with a roll of the eye, that her mother demanded she visit her aunts before returning to school. Rachel only shrugged. She didn't mind, given the tons of things she could do to fill her time. Besides, seeing Michelle turned out to be a bit of a downer.

But the tables turned for Michelle as she drove up 76 and saw a plane flying overhead. The sight of this Boeing jet gaining altitude lifted her spirits. All wasn't lost. She envisioned escaping them all; her mother's ridicule over the whole Brown thing, Rachel's new found happiness…and that damn Jill, plus the doom and gloom surrounding a nasty breakup. She always wanted to get away anyway. Forget two birds. She could kill three birds with one stone, and make money in route. Flight attendant, here she come!

Before turning onto Wissahickon she was speaking to a Delta employee telling her what she needed to do to get a job with the airline. "There's a real good flight program in Florida," suggested the woman who took her call. "And if you go to our site, there's a link to grants and loans you can apply for."

Cool beans. And they thought her back was on the ropes? God bless the woman who not only took her call, but answered her questions. She hopped online and got busy filling out forms and securing an 'instant' loan for $32K. This was enough money to pay her room and board and get her through one year of school in Florida. The classes weren't long…only a few hours a day, and probably easy too, which meant she could work part-time to pay for personal necessities, and maybe extras. The best news was, the next class started in two weeks, giving her time to do one more thing.

Get an abortion.

This was where she'd credit Julia, despite the praise not entirely a compliment. Her mother was the quintessence of making things happen. It was how she got into Brown, and too, how she escaped four years of guaranteed misery without forfeiting the tuition paid. Julia didn't play, and she never had to raise her voice or use threat tactics to make things go in her favor. Michelle wasn't as polished, what made her more determined to prove she wasn't a lost cause, or wasted effort, or even worse, a worthless child.

Luck still in business, she found the doctor who Rachel had gone to when she was in trouble. The man was still performing discreet abortions, without having to hand over health cards. Last thing she wanted to deal with was Julia riding her spirit seeing this procedure summarized on her insurance statement. Cash in hand, left over graduation money after buying school clothes and that airline ticket, Michelle made one pit stop before leaving out to see Dr. Jordan. She popped in on her mother, still brooding over the whole Brown ordeal, to wave her trump card in her face.

"Guess what ma'?"

Julia didn't look up. She was lounging on the chaise flipping through a magazine and in no mood to give her child another thing…not even advice.

"I'm going to flight school," Michelle announced showing all of her teeth.

"You're going where," Julia asked looking up.

"To flight school," Michelle repeated. "It's in Florida. I leave in two-weeks."

"Where—how did—"

"—Took care of everything ma'," she beamed, her proudest moment ever, the day when she proved to her mother she was a big girl after all. "I've been accepted, got my room assignment, and I'm leaving next Wednesday...so I have time to get situated—"

"—And just how are you going to pay for this flight school?"

"Got a 32K grant," she chirped like...NOW...TAKE THAT!

"A grant," Julia said sitting fully upright, swinging her legs off the chaise. "You mean 32 hundred, in a grant the school is giving you," —and without taking a breath she asked, "what's the name of the school?"

"Flight school...Academy of Flight School," Michelle replied a smidgen less confident. Just like that she had forgotten the name of the school and couldn't answer the second question because she didn't know the difference between a grant and a loan. Both terms were used on the forms she filled out.

"Let me see those forms," Julia pressed, about to rise up off the chaise.

"No mom, I gotta run. I have a doc—I mean I have an appointment. I'll show you all the paperwork when I get back."

"Did you just say you have a doctor's appointment?"

Things were spiraling fast out of control. This was what she so hated about her mother. She couldn't get nothing by her without this type grilling. It always got her so confused. "Yes," she replied flustered, fumbling with her purse. She was going for her car keys but found herself unzipping and opening compartments looking for an easy way to back out of what was supposed to be a clean wipe of her mother's face.

"I have to show proof I don't have—I mean, it's a drug test," she stammered. "They're checking for clean urine." Like Wow. Just Wow. That came out totally awkward. But she backed out of the room leaving her mother with her lips parted and eyes narrowed, telling her she'd be back in an hour.

Who was she kidding? It was going to take twice that long just to have the procedure. She drove to the clinic, a 3-story Graystone home located in the west part of the city. The house stood on the corner, in the same spot opposite a mom & pop deli selling cheesesteaks and hoagies she remembered several years ago. Parking was limited, typical, but nothing she had to deal with when her and Rachel last visited. They took the bus and a trolley. This time she parked up a hill about a block away. The doctor's assistant recommended she bring someone with her, but her fingers were crossed hoping all went well. Either way, whether she bled to death on a table in the clinic or at home, death was definitely on the menu if Julia found out she was pregnant.

The first sign of trouble appeared as she neared the clinic.

A group of Spanish-looking cuties rocking the slicked-back black hair and signature gangster attire were hanging out in front of the deli. It was about a dozen of them fanned out...some propped against the building, others leaning on cars and a few horse-playing in the middle of the street. It was going to be impossible to pass them without some sort of altercation; one of the worst predicaments a woman traveling alone in an inner-city neighborhood could encounter. It was akin to passing through (no pun intended) a den of wild dogs, wearing a pork chop hat and sausage coat.

Right away she pretended as if she'd forgotten something, and about faced, turning around to take a route that would add two extra blocks to her trip. But too late. One of the guys saw her, not that it was incredibly difficult to spot a lone female wearing suede leopard print pants, alligator 4-inch ankle boots, and a suede waist high jacket that allowed a primal view of one of her best assets.

The guy sprinted up the hill and caught up with her. "Hey mommie, why you tryin' to duck me?" he teased.

This was some primal instinct stuff going on here. He knew. This guy probably spotted her driving around the block looking for a parking space. He saw her pull into the space, and watched her check her mirror to ensure she was looking hot before hopping out of the car. He couldn't wait for her to approach, and likely too, knew just where she was headed.

She stopped and turned around. It couldn't be avoided... since she couldn't outrun him on 4-inches of shoe. And good luck trying to jump back in the car. She was parked on a one-way street. Either way she had to deal with this guy.

So, she smiled at the honey-colored cutie with the smart sexy eyes. "I didn't know you were trying to catch me," she replied, when her first thought was, 'man, he looks short.'

The guy laughed. "Aww...that's foul. Why you gonna do Vin like that?"

She didn't reply but kept walking, hair slinging and slaying, and hips bumping up and down, the whole while voices carrying on inside her head. Maybe she could knock on someone's door and he'd just go away. Nope. For some reason he didn't seem like the type. This guy looked like someone who'd stand at the door with her, and wait to hear her explain why she knocked on a stranger's door. That got her to thinking what he would say when he realized she had taken the long way to get where she was going. Maybe if she pulled a Forrest Gump, walking to Delaware or Jersey or straight down to the tip of Florida he would go away.

Those ramblings short lived, they didn't get to the corner before he asked where she was headed. "Don't tell me you was tryna' sneak around us to go see that butcher."

See. Smart eyes never lied. He knew, though she continued going the roundabout way, with him walking alongside. "So, you gone' make us walk this long ass way when we coulda' just went straight down the hill," he laughed. "I would-of' protected you," he added. "'Dem my boys. We wouldn't let nothin' happen to you."

Her heart had stopped racing. In fact, she couldn't detect a pulse at all. While the guy talked, and he talked a lot, she barely said a word. She smiled a lot though, and once or twice looked over at him to let him know she heard him, but he was doing all of the talking. For three full city blocks, completing about a 270-degree circle, he talked. At one point she happened to look up to see a crude sign handwritten in black marker on poster-size cardboard in the window. OB-GYN the sign read. In an instance she realized she had a pulse.

She almost choked, when he abruptly stopped and grabbed her arm. "So, you're really gonna let that butcher kill your kid!?"

Of course her mind was filled with responses. First of all, it was none of his business. Wasn't like it was his kid. Women and girls got abortions all the time. Rachel had one. It was no big deal. She cramped for a day, but a Tylenol later she was back at school the next day. The world was hardly going to miss one extra mouth no one wanted to feed. Besides, who was going to stop her…where the thoughts pumped the breaks.

"Look, I don't know you…yet," he halfway chuckled, more like cynically laughed. "But if 'dat was my kid in there," he said pointing at her midsection, "I'd kill that man if I found out he murdered one of my kids!"

"Well, this kid's father doesn't care," she meekly replied.

"Did you ask him? Does he know," this dude spat back, his mood exponentially changed.

Tears welled up in her eyes. She was scared more than anything. She really hadn't given abortion much thought. But this guy was forcing her to think… acting like she was about to murder an 8-pound baby in cold blood. If she had more time, she might've tried to come back later, when he and his boys weren't around. But she had just signed a $32K loan (or grant), and bought a $700 airline ticket. She didn't have that kind of time to play with.

"How about this," he said argumentatively. "I'm not letting you kill your kid!"

Now she was truly terrified. They stood facing each other, in a sort of stand-off, him transfixing her with a dark, cutting glare… and the grip he had on her arm. "I'm going to marry you, and take care of you and that kid," he told her.

Plot twist! She hadn't planned on a Vincent (aka Vin) Cabrera colliding into her life so brutally. She always imagined meeting the right guy for her, somewhat in the way she met Joshua, or better, guys like the one she fought Rachel over. This was how her and Rachel initially met. In 2nd grade there was this really cute boy, with the curly hair and long lashes who teachers were always sending to the office for disrupting class. He liked putting thumb tacks in teacher's chairs, or would crawl beneath desks to peek underneath dresses and skirts. His name was Lenny and everyone but teachers found him amusing.

Well, one day Michelle overheard Rachel talking about how Lenny tried to kiss her. But seriously!?! Just because Rachel was light skin didn't make her cute. The fact was, her mother let her eat too much sugar. She was the fattest girl in class, and she had a big fat head and fatter lips and nose. Rachel was tolerable to look at but she was NOT cute, even if her mother or someone in her house ever bothered to comb her bushy red hair. Michelle, for one, especially didn't want Lenny's name anywhere near her plus-size marshmallow pie looking lips. So, she spun around and spat, "I don't know why you're talking about him! He don't want you! In fact, don't no boy want a fat ass bitch like you!"

Classmates 'ooed and awed' while Rachel turned red as a beet. Both ended up locking arms and rolling around on the ground. As it happened to be, Rachel was wearing a dress, so everyone got to see her panties, an episode that would lead all the way up to her making out with her 6th grade teacher. By the end of that day however, they made up and Lenny merely became a caricature of the bad boys they crushed on; cute, not bashful, and exhibiting natural high levels of testosterone. Boys who might one day bring her roses and get down on one knee, perhaps Valentine's Day, and place one chunky 'blow your eyes out' diamond on her finger.

That's kind of how she fell for the five-and-a-half-foot tall guy with death-rays for eyes, and possible lethal weapon in his pocket. They talked for an hour outside the abortion place, him asking about her people, and she telling him about Joshua and Brown, and the 32K loan.

"That's what's wrong with the fucking world today," he spewed. "People like your mom thinking she free 'cause she don't see the shackles and got a big time job, teaching her kid to believe in the same bullshit!"

Whoa...she definitely wasn't taking this guy to meet Julia no time soon. And as they continued talking, him doing most of the soapbox orating and her answering his questions, she realized it might be the last time she saw her mother as well.

Just like that the Florida trip was off. She didn't dare return home, or so much as call Julia to explain her change in plans. Instead, she snaked her way through the city following Vincent to a house stuck between a row of homes raining people.

Two o'clock in the afternoon, mid-week, when most people were either in school or at work, or should have been in school or at work, this neighborhood looked like BoyzIIMen were holding a 'back home again' concert.

"Whad' up Vin? Who 'dat," someone asked.

"Mind ya' business. Don't be worrying about who 'dis is," Vincent replied.

She didn't look over to see who he was speaking to. She focused on what was right in front of her, a small step leading to a gawdy living room held hostage by velvet couches, diamond cut floor to ceiling mirrors, and a lone oil painting of Jesus hanging on a white wall leading upstairs. Her mother was going to die.

"Don't worry about any stuff you had at your moms," he told her. "I'm going to get you set up with new stuff so you don't have to go back there and get in a fight with her. You don't need to be dealing with 'dat right now."

He was saying the right things, but her ballot was still out to vote. It was much too early to tell if she made the right decision. In her mother's house the sink was two large stainless-steel basins, not one large white bowl in need of bleach, or maybe a harsh sanding and paint job. Also, she slept on a comfy plump 15-inch Sierra-Sleep mattress, not a lumpy 6-inch pad. The good thing was at least Vincent could tell by how she sat on the edge of the bed looking around the room that the promises he made needed to happen sooner than later.

So, he drove her to Ross's where she shopped for necessities like toiletries and bedding and nighties to sleep in. Small things, stuff to get by on, as he talked and talked about big things she wanted to know...such as his age, and if he had any children, or a girlfriend? Turned out he was 37, and had at least 19 children (that he knew of...) but no steady girlfriend, or wife. His first wife he lost, when he was twenty. The others ran off. Left him. He said most of them ran off to be with their first love...drugs. But there was one who moved to California, and took his kids. Another lived in Jersey, again with his kids. He only had his two youngest, living right next door with his mother! Segil, he said, was 15, and Amora was 12. Their mother was incarcerated.

"She's gonna be in there for a while," he said. "She messed up real bad."

Oh LORD. Poor Julia wasn't going to make it to her next birthday, which was in a few days. She was going to die of a lip chewing event if she heard this.

"That's all you need," he asked when she started pushing the cart towards the register.

She looked at the cart, piled to the top, with bedding stuffed beneath the cart. This she could get used to. When she went shopping with Julia, she had to buy the things she wanted using her own debit card. Of course, Julia bought all the food and household things like bedding. But still, she never got to walk around a store throwing whatever she wanted in the cart.

Later that evening she called her mother however, to let her know she was okay but wasn't coming 'back' home.

"Where are you," Julia snapped.

"Mom, don't worry about where I am. I just wanted to give you the courtesy of a call to let you know—"

"—Wren! Where are you!?!" Julia snapped again, sounding like a hissing snake.

Vincent, standing over her, took the phone. "Ugh, Mizz Perkins, Vin here. Your daughter is staying wif' me. She got a little situation going on that I'm going to deal with. You're welcome!" And he ended the call.

6...

Well! As can be imagined, the call shook Julia up. She gave birth to Michelle. Raised her. Had known her all of her life. Since when does some bum tell her to mind her business. Wren was HER business!

She closed the magazine laying open on her lap and slammed it on the nightstand and immediately called the police. "I need to report an abduction," she seethed into the phone.

The officer who took the call calmly asked a barrage of questions, almost sounding bored. Julia answered them all, in one-to-two-word clips, no more than three. The officer liked her style, being so direct and not acting overly emotional, like many parents of missing (or exploited) children. This lady meant business, though there wasn't much he could do. Michelle was 18. She had a right to up and leave home. He could however, trace Michelle's cell phone and GPS attached to her car, to notify the Philadelphia police department to do a welfare check.

A few days later Officer Pasquale knocked on Vincent's door, after knocking on other doors asking if anyone knew who owned the black Acura. Vogal, Vincent's mother, pointed right next door.

"I'm fine," Michelle told the officer. "My mother is just overly protective."

Pasquale ran his eyes up over the ceiling and around the gawdy living room before tossing her a cynical smirk. "Okay," he said, and he left.

Police gave Julia the scoop the following morning and for a week she dragged around her 3500-square feet of living space in a mental fog. This was a first for her. She only knew how to be one way. Mentally strong...and in control. Her own mother said she came out of the womb that way. Out of 13 children she was the only one born on her exact due date and gave her not a lick of trouble. She ate on schedule. Graduated on time. Completed college without returning home. Married according to tradition. And though she had Wren a later than customary, the successes she achieved throughout her career and marriage more than made up for the struggles she incurred becoming a mother so late. Julia was the family's steady rock.

Except now here she was, for the first time in her life, wading through a fog because her only child's spirit was gone. Just poof and gone. Before there'd been evidence of Michelle. A voicemail left on the house phone in her cheeky giggle. A piece of mail with her name on it. An unpaid bill. A photo on the mantle. Her spare car keys hanging on the corkboard in the kitchen. Even when she left for college her feisty spirit remained behind. There'd never been a moment when her spirit was so gone. It was like the child had died and taken her soul with her.

Lillian, her oldest sister, one of three still living, listened to her kid sister who she admired for keeping it so together, describe her daughter's spirit, mumbling about loans and feelings, and how she was too old to care for a grandchild. Wait? A What? Did she say a grandchild!?! Lillian liked to have fallen out of her chair, and this was no routine chair she sat in. It took gripping two high arm-rests and hanging on for dear life before she could hoist herself out of that chair.

Several times she jiggled her pinky inside her ear thinking she had a wax build up. She had heard about the Brown ordeal and how Michelle still had some growing up to do...as if she returned home because she was afraid of the dark. She didn't tell her baby sister as much, but Michelle was hardly Ivy League material. And having a baby!?! First thing that came to mind was Julia conveniently, as usual, left that part out. And yet, most shocking was hearing her sister moaning. This was NOT Julia Edafae Wright-Perkins. Julia Edafae never talked about feelings and emotions and being 'so' disappointed and 'utterly' depressed, and how she 'felt like' dying!

Lillian never drove anywhere 10 at night. Not at 72. And especially not if it included driving over one of them raggedy bridges to get there. But she was desperate to see her sister and no one cared to drive her from Delaware to Chestnut Hill. Julia was very particular about who she let in her space. She'd make them wait outside. In 30 years, the entire time Julia lived in that house, and even with family, to include her own mother, they were only invited as far as the patio, and they had to enter through the side gate. No one was allowed on Julia Edafae's white carpets, except her big sis.

Shaken by the disturbing call she drove to Chestnut Hill alone, all 110 miles, rattling and shaking the entire two-and-a-half hours with both hands on the steering wheel and eyes peeled so far apart that it looked like she was seeing through one huge eye ball.

Thanking God like she never praised Him before, she pulled up in the driveway to find Julia's little red Honda SUV parked in its normal spot. Michelle's Acura was nowhere in sight, which was eerie in some respects. Before Michelle left for Brown, it seemed like every other night Julia called to gripe about Michelle crushing her barberries and canna lilies. That garden was Julia's pride and joy, one of the most beautiful in the neighborhood, and Michelle seemed to take great pleasure rolling all four tires over the flower bed like a part of the asphalt.

Lillian knocked on the door anxious to see what state she'd find her sister in. She hoped for the best and was relieved when Julia opened the door looking like she last remembered her; prim and soft with very few wrinkles and her head wrapped in a white towel as if she'd just hopped out of the shower.

But this relief was short lived when Julia fell into her arms and burst out crying. "Out of all the years I've known that child, not once has she given me this much trouble," she sobbed.

Lillian begged to differ but wouldn't dare say it. The entire family had very few good things to say about a child they thought was born to a mother much too late. Julia was 45-years-old when Michelle was born. There were no other siblings, resulting in a child that was fawned over and coddled 24/7.

Michelle was breast fed until she almost started school. The girl had a full rack of teeth, top and bottom. The pouty mouth child was never anyone's favorite. No one except Julia, and big Joe who especially pampered the brat with thousand-dollar birthday parties, and Christmas gifts often imported from other countries, dressing her in cashmere coats with mink collars for Easter, and never EVER holding her accountable for anything.

Everything was always a mistake or an accident or someone else's fault, like the time she ruined Thanksgiving, yanking Mosely's, that would be her grandmother's table cloth straight off the table. Perry, their younger and more citified sister had to leave the house she was so tempted to beat up both her sister and niece when she heard Julia claiming the girl was trying to catch her balance to keep from falling. First of all, the child was 10! And secondly, they saw Michelle intentionally yank the table cloth, and giggle afterwards.

But Julia might've been right about one thing. Michelle hadn't ever been in serious legal trouble...that anyone knew of. Yet this wasn't saying a whole lot when living in a city (and surrounding areas where Michelle grew up), touting crime rates that exceeded 95% of national statistics, and ranking on international indexes. Because she hadn't murdered anyone (as far as anyone knew), or committed any major heists, or transported any major amounts of drugs... yet, was a moot point above the good ass-whipping everyone who knew her wanted to personally administer.

"Oh sis, sometimes we have to let them fall," Lillian chuckled. "You remember what mama used to say," she smiled, thinking back, softly stroking Julia's hand. "'...Don't nobody know the weight of water until they got to carry their own pail!'"

But Julia was hardly listening, one of her strongest attributes. She was staring at a pile of papers she had spread across the table. These were loan forms and flight school applications she found in Michelle's room. "It makes no sense she would take out this loan and then run off like she did," she huffed. "This is so irresponsible. I don't know how she's going to repay this money," she grumbled, mostly arguing with herself. "I just don't get it! Like, why!?! Something has to be wrong."

Lillian knew why, and definitely 'got it,' but kept her harshest criticisms to herself. Last time she lent her thoughts, after Michelle stole her car and narrowly missed killing a mother and her infant child, they didn't speak for months.

"Well, I talked to Perry last night and she said Bussy saw Wren," she casually replied, instantly snaring her sister's attention. Bussy was Perry's son, their nephew. He was several years older than Michelle, but while the cousins did know each other, they weren't close. "Perry said he saw her in Wawa, and she looked alright to him," Lillian added.

"Well, did he talk to her...what did she say..." Julia gushed before dashing off to grab her phone. In a never-mind fashion she called Perry, nearly one or two in the morning by this time, and without a greeting asked why hadn't she mentioned anything about Bussy seeing Wren, and asked for Bussy's number.

Perry, their middle sister, the sibling a few years younger than Julia who didn't mind stomping on feelings and butts, lifted up off her pillow and looked at the clock. "Julia, have you lost your mind," she greeted back. "Where are you? It's almost three in the morning!"

"Pear, I don't care what time it is. I think Michelle is in danger and I need—"

"—Whoa," Perry interrupted, leaving her bed so that she didn't disturb her husband, Carl. She left the bedroom and entered the bathroom, closing the door behind her so she could properly give Julia a piece of her mind. "You don't need to be asking about Bussy! You need to be talking to the police! Have you called them?"

"I have," Julia replied. "But you know they can't do anything because she's 18."

"Well, what's Bussy going to do? That girl don't listen to nobody! Never did. You know that!"

Julia was not used to being spoken to in this manner, because she stayed in her corner of the suburbs conversing with people who spoke her language. Rarely did she deal with family, especially Perry, who lived, as often joked, in the hood. Thirty-forty years ago she had put Cedar Avenue, right below 62nd Street, in her past...well behind her.

Perry, however, was bringing her big sister back to West Philly, closer to her reality. "What you need to do is get off your high horse and put on some steel toe Uggs and put your foot where it should have been when that girl was busting up mama's China," she railed on. "She's down there around 16th & Girard with them Cubanos," she said, adding for a sign off, "good luck!"

Julia was aghast, though the pep spiel brought her out of the fog. After all, that's what sisters are for. She looked down at Lillian and flatly said, "I'm done. I gave that child everything. Can't say I didn't try my best. The rest is on God."

But there was one person who hadn't given up on Michelle. For two weeks Rachel had been blowing up Michelle's cellphone. Usually they talked every other night. But Michelle wasn't answering her calls. The first couple of nights when this happened, Rachel thought Michelle might've gotten a little salty over the whole Jill thing. It wasn't the first time they got into a tiff over one or the other breaking one of their unwritten rules. When that happened, they wouldn't speak for a couple of days, but this had been 14 whole days...the longest they'd gone without zero communication.

   She started to make travel arrangements with Jill anyway, to surprise Michelle with a visit. She didn't have to know how she got there. All she needed to know was she WAS there. But she got concerned when on one call she learned Michelle's phone number was no longer in service. So, she called Mrs. Perkins, something she had never done.

   Despite knowing Michelle's mom, almost as long as she'd known Michelle, neither were fond of the other. Or, perhaps more like it, Rachel agreed with Michelle. She hated Mrs. Perkins. She thought Julia put too much pressure on her friend. Ridiculous rules like making Michelle give her two-weeks-notice before she could schedule a sleepover. And she couldn't talk on the phone after 8PM. Like what sane parent in the late 90's and early 2000's enforced those ancient 80's grandparent rules!?!

   Michelle could only see Rated-PG movies, and rap music was forbidden in her home. Also, Julia had this really weird rule. She had to meet the parents of every single one of Michelle's friends before she could associate with them. Fortunately, they met in 2nd grade, when both her parents were married and living together. Otherwise, they may have never become friends, the main reason

Rachel really hated Julia. When her mom upped and left, Julia tried to sever the friendship by curtailing the time they could spend together, which was limited to begin with. For a whole year they snuck around like cheating spouses. Eventually Julia lifted her nasty little ban, when Michelle pressed the issue, calling her mother a hypocrite. Just because her father was dead, didn't make her better than Mr. Jackson who was divorced. A one-parent household, was a one-parent household! Julia caved, with one exception. The sleepover ban she continued to enforce, until the day they left for college.

But Rachel was desperate. She had to know what happened to Shelly. Regardless, that girl was her ride or die. She loved her like a true sister. They had traded blood, kept big secrets, snuck into R-rated movies anyway, and once even discussed killing Julia... and their plans for concealing the crime. They were besties for life. She'd walk to the end of earth for Shelly!

The call, though, was brief, and very, very chilly. Julia told her, and quite bluntly, Michelle had moved on with her life.

Rachel was stunned. Totally and holistically stunned. She was so shocked and speechless that she called Julia right back.

"...Umm, Mrs. Perkins, what do you mean Michelle moved on? I'm about to visit her at school, but her phone is disconnected."

"Michelle is no longer at school. She's living with some bum in North Philly," she tersely replied, along with a few other choice thoughts that ended with her suggesting that she forget about her friend and move on with her life too!

Rachel practically had to scrape her lip off the floor. She would've probed more, except, and as usual, Julia sounded intolerably irritated. So, she took her anxiety to a classmate she befriended, Joe Delgado.

"Go to Student Affairs," Joe told her. "Ask for Amy."

Rachel didn't ask why, or more aptly, how Amy might help in this situation. It wasn't as if Michelle was affiliated with the college. In fact, according to Julia, Michelle was no longer affiliated with any school. But Rachel trusted Joe, unassailably.

The 'short stack', as she was dubbed on the streets of Chicago, knew her way around. The five-foot-two feisty firecracker and first year Penn student knew all the popular hole-in-a-wall locations where they could drink, smoke and throw down their half-baked rhetoric and cheeky rhymes.

Also, Joe was good with campus guards. They'd let her in classrooms after hours to hold open mic slams. Cool with the street crowd, she'd invite rappers and hood-types to 'take out the trash,' a muse that described showing 'wannabes' sophistocated techniques of mixing words with lyrics and making music. The wildly diverse word art festivals she organized influenced many, to include upper classmen. The girl, already branded, was a natural boss, and this was the real kicker. Other than orientation she hadn't stepped foot in Philly before, and claimed to only be 17-years-old! So, if Joe said 'go see Amy', then she went to go see Amy.

Skipping classes that day Rachel popped in the Student Affairs suite and asked for Amy. She was directed towards a heavyset woman much too large for her chair, stuffed in a cubicle hunched over a bag of Doritos. Crumbs were everywhere, and it was nine in the morning.

Suddenly, the idea of pouring out her heart to a woman who didn't seem to care much about her health seemed absurd. The scene she walked over to made her think twice about why she was there. After all, it was Michelle who stopped answering her calls, which of all offenses, she clearly had been lying if, as her mother revealed, she dropped out of Brown before her visit to Penn. But she was too slow inventing the story for why, first thing in the morning she walked across campus, skipping class, to show up in Student Affairs specifically asking to speak to a woman with unhealthy eating habits.

"What's up, doll?" Amy cackled in a plump buzz kill voice, sounding like she'd been up all night, refereeing pity parties. "Pull over a chair," she said amused.

For a second, Rachel stammered. She'd forgotten how she planned to open the dialogue. "My friend," was as much as she managed to get out.

And there again came the buzz kill voice. "So, you got a friend," Amy chuckled, raising two clubby fingers to simulate quotes. "I got a friend too. Hell, I got lots of friends," she laughed, apparently thinking she was funny mimicking a dusty line from the popular 90's gun-slinger flick, 'Tombstone.'

Though Rachel sheepishly grinned, she wasn't amused. She suspected her bestie of possibly being caught up in a sex-trafficking situation, and voiced those suspicions.

"—Wait," Amy broke in, bouncing once in the chair before swiveling around to face her. "You really believe that," she said as agape as Rachel had been hearing Michelle had left Brown.

"Yes," Rachel replied, her voice stiff and starchy. For Christ's sake her sweet, innocent beautiful bestie left school, and not just any school, but the prestigious Brown University. According to Julia, she moved in with a true real life bad boy.

But Rachel wasn't getting a pleasant feel from this Amy. She got the distinct impression Amy not only didn't believe her, but was playing her for a fool. Naive she might have been, but she was a a product of Philadelphia too. For a minute however, she even began to doubt the authenticity of Joe's street creds.

But then Amy did something that encouraged her to stay the course. As she bent over to pick up a Dorrito that had fallen to the floor, a small caliber gun popped from between her cleavage. Rachel's eyes went straight to the tiny silver gun, no bigger than an early generation flip phone, landing on the floor, right beside Amy's left croc. Like a city crook seeing an unattended bill, Amy scooped up the weapon and slipped it back in its nook. But Rachel's eyes had twisted left-wise and landed on a book laying near the Doritos bag by the time the student affairs advisor lifted up.

"You didn't see that," Amy asked, pushing her Potter rims up the bridge of her nose.

"See what," Rachel asked, this quick response coming out as natural as accidental. By this time, she was looking at a copy of 'Lovely Bones', flipped over and parted open to where Amy had stopped reading. "I wanted to read that novel," she said nodding towards the book. "...But I think I'm going to wait for the movie to come out," she added.

Amy gasped, patting the part where the little silver nugget had disappeared. "Oh my God! You're breaking my heart," she sighed. "I can guarantee you the book will be much better!"

Rachel didn't object, even if it made no sense that Amy could predict something like that. "The thing is," she continued anyways, "...police are refusing to help because this girl is 18...but I saw her the week she dropped out of Brown. She looked awful, like she was being watched, or owed somebody money."

"Really," Amy asked, bringing a chip to her lips as if she was reading the greatest thriller of all times. "You saw all this..."

Rachel didn't know any of this for fact. It was a little bit of amateur sleuth work she had done merging what she knew with what Julia told her. Yet, oblivious to Amy's sarcasm she went on explaining how strange Michelle acted; the bathroom trips, not eating, and making an excuse to cut their visit short. "This just wasn't the friend I'd known my whole life," she concluded.

"Sounds like your friend was embarrassed. She probably got knocked up. It happens all the time," Amy said like nothing.

"—And so, I should just forget about her and let some—"

"—Hey, hey," Amy interjected, seeing a full-on melt down coming. Last thing she wanted was another student bawling in the suite and drawing the big shots out of their offices.

"I'm not saying that," she urgently whispered. "I know sex-trafficking is a real thing...just give me a couple of days and we'll get to the bottom of it."

Rachel left the department feeling 1000% better, not saying much since before she got there she felt 5000% sure a part of her was dying. But she was relieved Amy liked reading, and not only liked books related to solving mysteries, but the gun-slinger loved reading high-brow sleuth novels, period!

And still, she returned to her dorm unable to sleep, eat and certainly in no mood to attend classes during the 26 hours she counted in seconds. Ten o'clock the following day Amy called. As promised, she dug up where Michelle was likely staying.

"Just so you know, you can find this info in the White Pages online," she carefully explained. "Just go to www dot locater dot com," she instructed. "Now, I advise you to speak with your parents before trying to contact your friend," she cautioned. "And definitely do not go anywhere, especially in the city, alone."

Amy knew her advice hadn't landed. Like 99.98% of students she advised to do this or the other, she'd later find out they did the exact opposite of the other and then tried to pin the blame on everyone but themselves. Enough battle scars peppered her personnel files that she knew to the very last line Rachel was going to type her friend's name into a search engine on her personal computer and go directly to that location, probably alone.

Well...okay. Almost.

Rachel wasn't that bold to travel to North Philly without company, especially knowing a bad boy lived there. She called her oldest sister, Kimberly, and shared her intentions. "Look, I'm going with you," Kim said. "You know how Michelle is. She'll freak out if you approach her with some random friend!"

8...

While her family and friends were losing their center, she was relatively okay. No, her situation wasn't ideal, but it was better than having to deal with her mother and being bored at home. Getting to know Vincent and his family was like visiting an amusement park and riding all the rides.

After taking her shopping, peeling off crisp hundred-dollar bills and slinging them across counters at cashiers in discount stores, he started laying out real cash, replacing the mirrors and velvet couches and kitchen appliances with textiles she could stand to look at. It was funny when she overheard a cousin groan, "damn Vin, you know you can't buy love, right?"

"Well, I'ma try," Vincent shot back. "I ain't lettin' 'dis one get away."

And that's just how it began for them. Tough as he projected himself, from the day she arrived he did his best to get her situated and comfortable. And so what he took her to cheap stores buying pjs and sweats, the kind of stuff she'd never wear in public. It was cool. With her waistline growing by the minute, those throwaways were going to come in handy. It wasn't like she was going to be pregnant forever, or at least she hoped not. More times than okay though, he mentioned sons he wanted to have; the one living with him, he wasn't too enamored with, so she was on notice.

That was the other funny thing, the swervy part of living with him. The day she moved in, was the day he told his brothers and cousins they had to stay next door...with Voge. Before, the family hopped back and forth across the banister, a long thin railing that separated the front porches. But Vincent declared those days were over. He moved them out and moved in his kids; Segil...his problem child who the family called lil Gil, and Amora...a tiny little girl with a diamond shaped face.

No one outright contested the new arrangement. The family seemed like they could lay their head anywhere and be fine. There were times when she'd return home from a shopping trip to find a cousin or brother curled up in a corner of the porch beneath a pile of quilts, sound asleep. It was damn near 32 degrees outside, craziness it took time to adjust to.

It also took her time to get used to lil Gil. The kid was kind of odd. He was 12, but didn't say much. He kept to himself, staying locked in his room playing video games. He only came out to eat, which he ate next door. In a way she couldn't blame him. Before his father threw out a relic white stove that likely came with the house when it was built a century ago, they were microwaving TV dinners, while Voge was next door burning meals, literally.

The scents that came through the cracks in the walls and windows, were the talk up and down the block. Even she, who was no fan of curry and Cajun food, talked about Voge's cooking. "Oh my God Vin, this is good!" She loved his mother's jerk chicken, which she made just about daily, along with some spicey ribs and crispy rice, and all kinds of pies, and cakes, and banana raisin-nut muffins. She hardly blamed lil Gil for hopping the banister to go next door to eat. It likely was why her waist was expanding by the minute. Soon as Vincent got home from his day of tearing down homes, or whatever odd jobs he had scheduled that day the first words out of her mouth would be, "oool Vin, go over there and bring me a plate of whatever Voge is cooking today!"

At any rate, lil Gil was strange. Far as she could tell, he didn't go to school, and she never saw him playing with friends. He kind of creeped her out. One night she got up to go to the bathroom and there he was, sitting on the stairs, with his head down and hands covering his ears. The next morning she mentioned it to Vincent. Maybe the kid didn't like his daddy sleeping with another woman. "Aww, he waitin' for his motha' to come home," Vincent replied. "He been doing 'dat shit since she got locked up."

Michelle didn't probe, because this was something she learned early about Vincent. Some things he didn't like talking about and would snap without warning. One time he came home pissed at his brother Paco for tearing up the roof of a truck they rented.

"I tol' 'dem knuckleheads not to stop at that damn dump in the first place," he lamented. "Their milkshakes taste like rotten milk and chicken ain't nothing but fried flour!"

His diction tickled her, so she giggled, when between re-telling what happened he yelled, "'dat shit ain't funny!"

She stopped smiling after that outburst, and let him retell

stories without showing a reaction. "I was like telling him," he continued worked up, snatching off his watch and slamming it on the dresser. "'Da damn thing wasn't gonna clear 'dat pole! But Pac kept sayin' whadtn' nobody gonna know if a little came off the top!'"

The story was just too funny, especially when a manager ran out frantically waving and yelling for them to stop. But then she got why Vincent didn't find the event laughable. Police came for them, and paramedics for the manager. Luckily they weren't detained long. The manager decided not to press charges, though Vincent was more pissed about having to come out of pocket to pay the fines.

Even so, she learned to enjoy Vincent's many stories wearing Poker faces... like a night he came home laughing about mom and pop deli owners that needed a couple of freezer removed. The couple's daughter was in the store when they arrived, which he thought the girl 'looked young' but noted she did have breasts. If he had to guess, she definitely was underage, but not a toddler. He didn't pay her much attention though, except for repeatedly having to ask her to move out of the doorway. They finished the job and were climbing in the truck when they heard the owner shouting at Salvatore (aka big Sal), one of the cousins. No one knew exactly when Sal was born, but he contracted polio at birth...and was slow. But the owners didn't know this, demanding that he apologize to their daughter because he had no business touching the child.

But Sal protested. "She touched me first!"

"But she's special," railed the owner.

"Well, I'm special too," Sal argued back.

Vincent laughed hard on that one, but she didn't. She smelled the brandy on his breath.

And yet, his mother was THE MOST intimidating aspect of living with him. The first time she met her, Voge was sitting in a rocker by the door staring out a window. She seemed so small and harmless, like a little old fragile lady that might fall over if she sneezed. But one step towards the dark shadow, she almost lost her balance when Voge's head, and nothing else, suddenly jerked around. Think Exorcist remake...except the beseiged was ten shades darker and had company. A black cat. Vincent, who broke her stumble, said it was 'Chenzo' that hissed at her. She disagreed, but let that brisket go.

"Ma'ma, 'dis is Che-Che. She's going to stay wif' me," he said to the woman who looked a hundred, going on a thousand, glaring at her from pulsating kale green eyes. She muttered something to him, and he told her to chill. "Li se bon fi, ou pral wè," he said before kissing her on the jaw.

Back home, next door, Vincent broke it down for her, telling her his mother had a hard life growing up in Havana. She had her first kid when she was thirteen, and got married when she was 18, when he was born. Raising a family early, and five boys at that, wasn't easy. But add farm work and witnessing a few murders and life was hell for her. Her husband, his father was killed when he was about 10, though that happened after moving to Florida, which was after living briefly in the Dominican Republic and Haiti. After the murder of his father they left Miami and moved to Harlem where his father's people lived.

But Voge, who had difficulty adjusting to America, didn't get along with the in-laws. It didn't sit right with them when she moved in with an alcoholic who gave her four more mouths to feed. Eventually eleven became ten, when the drunk put them out on the streets. A few homeless shelters later, where one of his sisters died of scarlet fever, they scraped together enough cash to board a bus that brought all nine of them to Philadelphia. Initially they rented the house Voge lived in, which in 1981 was little more than four walls and an umbrella for a roof. But he and his brothers fixed the place up, how they got their construction business started, and what helped buy the house next door a few years later. The family had been through a lot, but Voge had been through more.

"But don't worry," he told her. "So long as your heart stay good and you innocent and sweet like you are, Voge won't let nobody mess wif' you."

His words were hardly comforting. She was convinced his mother was reacting off bad energy emanating from her.

"...Naw," he assured her. "She jus' know how long I've been trying to find 'da right one. Every time I bring someone home, hoping 'dey're 'da one, 'dey get on 'dat stuff and lose 'dey mind."

And that really didn't help. With the craziness going on in her new life, it was possible she might get on the same stuff and lose her mind too. It was Amora however, his little bright-eyed doll with the bushy brows and infectious smile that changed her outlook.

Amora kept a diary, which she read an entry every night. Mostly she wrote about how lady bugs smelled like spaghetti, and the hum snowflakes made when falling, along with poems about fancy homes, nice people, and how her grandmother put her 'Barbie size feet' in food that tasted good as it looked.' Only one story darkened this journal. It had to be traumatizing to witness her mother dragged out of the house by police. She described her mother's hair in disarray. Normally she wore it styled, but that night, at 2:39AM (she noted), it was 'messed up'. They didn't wait for her to change out of her nightgown either. They got to see her undies...and parts of her peachacobbler...' a visual Rachel tried to erase as she listened to the docile voice describing a horrifying event like recalling a scene in a movie she thought somewhat sad. A child's innocence stolen by seeing her mom's private parts she still referred to as a 'peachacobbler', and noticing how one cop seemed pleased by this because he "had a hard-on," was plain alarming.

But if a 9-year-old child could smell roses from a field of fresh fertilizer, and not frown, then an 18-year-old woman about to have a baby had no business complaining about an old woman, (which Voge was hardly old as she looked), possibly not liking her. Besides, Amora seemed to love her grandmother, mostly feeling sorry for who she called 'MyVogue'. 'People don't like her because they think she know maji and don't speak English.'

How could she not fall in love with a child who reasoned like this? A child who could look at a shriveled up hissing woman whose coral green coyote eyes glowed in the dark and see a soul worth admiring rather than an abyss to avoid, she'd dig her heels in for. And yet, she didn't take that final step until she overheard an argument between Vincent and his baby sister Fe-Fe.

Voge wasn't the only one who occasionally sat by the window. Sometimes she did too, upstairs in their bedroom watching and listening to the comings and goings of the family. They knew everyone on the block; neighbors, visitors, vagrants walking down the street, even people waving from passing cars. Listening to them clowning and telling stories was far more entertaining than reality TV. She couldn't get over how cars would be parked back-to-back up and down the block, squeezed in so tight that some would be hooked onto bumpers and grills, yet the 'unmarked' parking spots in front of the house remained empty. No cones or chairs necessary. The message was clear. Nobody, but the family, parked in front of Voge's and Vin's house. Respect them, and they returned the respect. Forget a security gate, the Cabreros was all the protection a community needed.

But every so often an unknown visitor might drop in and slide into one of the forbidden spots. This was what she assumed happened when she heard yelling. Initially she didn't see anyone, but heard his voice. Parked out front was her car, his truck and Fe-Fe's banged-up Cherokee Jeep. Since moving in Fe-Fe had been staying with a male friend. She was only 17, the real teller about how young Voge was, and another indicator of the family's values. OH GOODNESS!...that would mount his soapbox and stay on that box for a good while when it came to American values on family.

"Instead of encouraging 'deez kids to change 'dey gender, how 'bout lettin' them use it, to see if 'dey want to change it!"

He vehemently argued America had it backwards. First of all, the family was Catholic, a bit of a surprise for her. They believed building families came first, then college and career. Young people needed to get married, raise a family and gather life experiences before running out in the world trying to save it without having any concept of working through real problems. "That's the reason shit is so fucked up," he contended.

Suffice to say, Fe-Fe living with a man at seventeen was no big deal. In fact, she was applauded. So when Michelle opened the window to see who he was arguing with, and saw it was Fe-Fe, she quickly closed the window. Besides the fact it was cold out, she didn't want to be caught eavesdropping. There was no telling what he was on his soapbox ranting about, but he was very sensitive when it came to family.

About 40-minutes later Fe-Fe poked her head in the room. "Hey," she softly said. "I just wanted to let you know I'll be leaving and probably won't see you guys for a while..."

Shocked and saddened, Michelle asked where she was going. Fe-Fe was instrumental in helping her settle into the family. "Girl, I'm just so glad you're here," she told her one day like a tired mother relieved the sitter had finally shown up. "Voge can't watch that girl," she said speaking of Amora who she had been playing mother to since the child's birth.

Naturally Vincent was pissed about Fe-Fe announcing she was joining the Army. "The only reason I didn't join sooner was because I didn't want to see him going to prison for killing one of them knuckleheads he have hanging around here," she muttered.

It was a Saturday afternoon, almost four months into Michelle's disappearance when Rachel and her sister Kim finally coordinated their schedules to visit the home on Thompson Street. Whatever the conveniences for why they chose that specific day, it was the worst possible day they could have selected. Not only was the entire family home, but that weekend they were barbecuing…and the family, to include Vincent, had started drinking.

Michelle was upstairs combing Amora's hair when she heard the knock on the door. Normally no one knocked, because normally, especially during the day, no one came up those steps that wasn't either a delivery person or knew the door was unlocked. On rare occasions there'd be a brave solicitor wandering the neighborhood. Most times employees of Comcast or Verizon who came with company vehicles and backup. Overall the family hopped the railing stopping visitors on the porch so that there was no need to knock. So, she peeked over her shoulder out of the window to see if there were any unusual vehicles or activities. Police visiting was another possibility. Since she'd been there it hadn't happened a lot, but there had been a couple judicial-related visits…once looking for Sal who was staying with relatives in Brooklyn, and another time to pick up Luis, the brother a year older than Vincent, still serving time for crimes he committed.

But Michelle didn't see anything unusual. So she continued fixing Amora's hair, teasing her Afro puffs and brushing her edges into swirls. Suddenly Vincent broke the ambiance yelling upstairs.

"Che-Che, you got some visitors!"

Michelle froze. She wondered aloud who that could be. 'Don't tell me Julia Edafae got the gumption to come out here," she muttered a little panicked.

"Who's Julia," Amora asked.

"My mother," she replied.

"You got a mother," Amora asked amused. She didn't mean it like it sounded. It was just that Michelle never talked about her mother, or family for that matter. She walked into their lives like an orphan that had escaped one of too many situations written about on the next to the last page in newspapers.

"Do me a favor," Michelle said to Amora. "Go downstairs and see who it is."

"Alright, I'ma yell it stinks down here, if it's some smokies down there," she said, rehearsed in the drill.

Of course Michelle was not worried about police. They'd already done their welfare check and hadn't been back since. She just wanted a clue to who had come asking for her so that she could prepare her attitude.

In a flash Amora disappeared. In socks she skipped down the stairs as if they were a slide. "It stinks down here," she yelled back up the stairs.

Concerned, Michelle dropped the brush on the dresser and headed downstairs herself. She had a tongue-lashing ready for the cop who let Julia twist his (or her) arm behind their back. But around the second step down she heard Vincent tell his daughter to go sit her tail at the table and eat the breakfast he cooked. "... And what I tell you 'bout slippin' and slidin' around in 'dem socks," he fussed. "You gone' break your neck. Chee-Cheee," he yelled again, as she had already made it to the middle landing of the stairs.

Only able to see from the knees down she knew it was two women, but not Julia. These women were younger, and not so fancy dressed. Julia never wore jeans and white sneaker boots, and didn't hang around anyone who did.

When Rachel and her sister Kim came into full view she smiled. It seemed like ages since she'd seen her old friend, and even more ages since she'd seen her old friend and sister together. But she had no time to see where Vincent was, or if anyone else was in the front room because Rachel immediately ran over to the stairs. "Shell—Shelly," she dramatically gasped, "what's going on? Are you okay," she cried.

And that's when she heard him. "What the fuck you mean why she here," he snarled.

It wasn't even 9AM. Voge probably had just put the ground beef in a bowl and covered it with plastic wrap. She could see her pulling spices from her overcrowded cabinet, and fussing with Sergio or Tony or one of her nephews to make sure the coals were burning. It was about 32 degrees out and she didn't care if they had to chop up that brand new 10K deck they built to keep that grill hot, she was cu'ing everything in the fridge. Shrimp, crabs, clams, oysters, mussels, burgers, ribs, tofu...and especially the chicken...all of it, plus the joumou and the cassava was either getting grill marks, smoke flavor or both...whether everybody in the house was already full of alcohol or not.

"Rocky, let's go," Kim said standing by the door, splitting her attention between anticipating Vincent's next move, stealing glances at Michelle, and watching her sister.

"No," Vincent shouted, his speech slurred some. "I first want to know what she mean by is she okay!"

Hearing the commotion little Amora rushed into the front room, and seeing her father moving towards Rachel with a bottle in his hand she slid in front of him. "No, daddy, don't..." she said wrapping her arms around his waist. "Don't do it daddy, they're not worth it."

Kim left Vincent's home irritated. "We probably could've gotten her to come outside had you not gone in there acting like Jesus Christ the superstar," she scolded Rachel on the way to her car. "You have to learn how to control your emotions."

"What!?! What are you talking about," Rachel shrieked. Kim might've been older, 16 years older in fact, but in the 11 years she'd been working with the school board she was still an admin making less than 50K a year. Maybe she was too in control of her emotions? Perhaps it was time she started raising her voice and stop making excuses for why she hadn't once been promoted!

"I'm saying you have to learn some diplomacy, how to suck up—"

"—What!?!" Rachel shrieked again. Exactly Kim's problem. Why she was stuck in a house she couldn't afford, making ends meet with two children, no husband and a dead-end job. "Well, I don't kiss ass, I kick ass," she slammed back.

Kim laughed, mockingly. Rachel hadn't fought anyone since second grade when she got into the little tiff with the other little Miss Sheltered. Neither one of them surfaced to mind when it came to recruiting real fighters. Both of them, the most whimsical kids in America, were all puff, no bite. "Well, if you're trying to help Shelly, you're going to have to win her confidence."

Win her confidence? Why? For what!?! "That's the most ridiculous thing I ever heard," Rachel spewed. "Why would anyone in their right mind need to be begged to leave a situation like that!?! If it was me—"

"—But that's just it Rocky. It's not you—"

"—Well, I know Shelly," she fumed. "She'd never live in a dump like that! Did you see those tacky paintings on the walls?! And, UGH...them nasty pillows on that throw-up looking couch!

It's no way you can tell me she's living in something like that on her free will! I know she's being held hostage! I just know it!"

Kim had seen it. She was right there. She saw it all. The drab living room. The Bohemian furniture. The clear to the back of the house, ratty kitchen. And the plethora of red-eyed bums already sauced up at 9AM. She thought for sure they were going to intervene, or let Vincent go. He really got wild when they rushed into the house, slipping and falling and stumbling out of the house to get at them. He did throw the bottle at them, but she already had the car started and both doors locked. "But I didn't see no tape on her mouth," she shot back.

That's when Rachel lost it. By the time the sisters reached the campus they were shouting at each other. Not that Kim had anything against Michelle, aside from thinking she was eccentric and liked her sister in a lesbian way, but she wasn't as invested in her drama. The girl looked alright to her. She certainly hadn't lost any weight. And at least she was alive. Besides, Rachel was right about one thing. She had two kids at home in need of eating, and a job she had to put up with to make ends meet since her ex-husband was more interested in showing off his new family than taking care of his old one. Happily she let the ball of hot air bail out of her car. Good riddance! Go! "Let me know how the saga ends," she hurled onto 36th Street before her hotheaded sister slammed the door shut.

Rachel marched straight to Joe's dorm and interrupted her early afternoon session entertaining a male suitor. "So, I found her," she huffed, ignoring two blank stares and a disturbingly disheveled bed. It looked like Joe and her friend also could have been rehearsing a mock trial. Both were fully dressed, however sloppily and rumpled, and standing upright and apart from one another, but it looked like they were in the middle of something.

"You found who," Joe asked.

"You remember, my friend," Rachel replied like Joe was the stupid one.

"Oh, yeah," she remembered, discreetly rolling her eyes as she turned away, headed to her small kitchen table following her friend. "Was she okay?"

"No," Rachel snapped. "That's why I'm here. She's staying in a crack house with some drug dealers. I think she's scared. I couldn't get her to leave with me..." and she burst out crying, heaving and sobbing, trying to explain the plea she read in Michelle's eye, and how they grew up together, and how pretty she used to be, and how fat she had gotten. "I can't believe it! And nobody is doing a thing about it," she sobbed in her hands.

Joe sat in her friend's lap, looking just as aloof. The story sounded intriguing, as if Rachel had burst in describing a bloody car accident she passed on the way over. There was just nothing either of them could do for Michelle, or Rachel, except maybe hand her a tissue, which a roll of paper towels was within inches of their elbows. Yet neither bothered to so much as pull one sheet from the roll and hand it to her to wipe her face.

"Well, at least you know where she is..." Joe replied as if talking on eggshells.

That's when Rachel noticed the guy's leg quivering, just as he saw her noticing. Abruptly he stopped his leg and sat stiff as a board, which alerted Joe she needed to quickly come up with something to get Rachel on her way. "Hey, I know," she exclaimed, without popping up. "Why don't you invite her to 'Last Call'? They're holding one on Front Street, at the Warehouse tonight."

Nice try, but no good. Michelle had changed her number and she would be on her way to hell before she'd step foot in a warehouse she almost lost her life in. Instead, she left the lovers and returned to her dorm where she caught up with Amy, on the phone, who was busy too. The armed mystery reader had guests over. Incredibly rude guests, as Rachel could hear them in the background. One even interrupted their conversation, clearly seeing Amy was on the phone, asking where she kept her hot sauce. Really!?! Hot sauce!?! This rudeness may have been forgivable had this person not continued asking for things, and had Amy not kept cutting her off to answer the person. The salvageable part of the conversation was Amy agreeing to talk more, sometime Monday.

So she rubbed her knuckles waiting for Saturday to finish, and Sunday to come and go. Eight AM sharp, first thing Monday on a bone-chilling freezing morning, she stood outside the Student Affairs office waiting for Amy to stop by Starbucks before walking across the quad, shivering and shaking in a wool coat, mittens, earmuffs and juggling coffee and bags large enough to hold Barnes & Noble inside...to meet her as promised.

Soon as Amy appeared, she started talking. "I don't know if you heard me the other night, but I finally found her!"

"Great," Amy replied, juggling a workbag, purse, keys and coffee using her chin, shoulder and one hand. "Is she okay," she asked, already knowing the answer. The front of her day would've started much less annoying if Rachel knew unequivocally Michelle was NOT okay. Out of all the people up and moving about on that frost-biting morning, Michelle likely was the warmest and most comfortable, sleeping soundly beneath a big fluffy comforter, probably with that man nestled up to her. If only people like Rachel realized these things, the world would be so much happier!

Juggling the purse, workbag and coffee Amy opened the door, turned on lights and told Rachel to pull over a chair…she'd be with her in a minute. The minute though, took more like half an hour, which Rachel saw every passing minute like the parent of a missing child pained with worry wondering where their child was, or what she (or he) was eating, and if the child was hurting, or in pain, or crying out for their mommy or daddy. By the time Amy finally plopped down in her springy chair with the giant whoosh, and pulled up to her 'had to be' ice-cold coffee, Rachel was breathing like a fire dragon.

"So, what time is your next class," Amy asked, having solved the case Rachel was chasing when she first met her.

But Rachel looked at the woman like she was watching an octopus using all eight tentacles to slap rain. Like, what kind of question was that? She started to answer, and not so kind, but Amy popped up out of the chair excusing herself again. This time she needed to reheat her coffee.

A few minutes later she was back, plopping back down in the chair and twirling around to face her computer. She removed her clubby dimpled paws from around the paper cup to poke at the keyboard, using one finger on the keyboard as if counting dots on a domino chip. With the other hand she took careful slow sips of her coffee, watching the screen dispassionately. All of this would have looked normal had Rachel not been sitting there…waiting.

After what seemed like watching pages on a calendar flip over Amy finally rotated her screen around and invited Rachel to move closer. "Is this him? Is this the guy you saw with your friend?"

Rachel looked at the screen. She didn't have to squint. Amy had been thoughtful enough to enlarge the image to fill her screen. She recognized him right away. It was him, though what took her breath away was the rap sheet she scanned with her eyes opened wide as they could spread following the bold print. **Felony Assault. Aggravated Robbery. Attempted Assault.** And what knocked the wind out of her sail was stopping at that one word. **MURDER.** "Oh my God," she muttered covering her mouth.

Her turn. She popped up out of the chair, knowing just where she was headed when Amy stopped her. "Hold on," she said. "There's no sense in running to police. Your friend's mother has already alerted them, and police have already been to the house. But you can do something," she quietly tendered. "Talk with your Ethics Professor about taking on a research project that involves abusive relationships. She does a lot of work in that area."

But Rachel didn't have time for no long-ass research project. Her friend as they spoke lived with a convicted MURDERER!

Was this woman...this supposed adviser...on DRUGS!?! "Why are we wasting time here," she angrily blurted. "Don't you realize Shelly's life is in danger? Why can't NO ONE NOT see this!?!"

"—Whoa...hold up Lethal Weapon II," Amy cut in. "Let's take a deep breath...and one step at a time. I know you want to go in there all gangbusters and drag your friend out as if the house is burning down, but you could be doing your friend more harm than good," she said before throwing some scientific logic at her. "Did you know that the fix to helping someone dying of starvation is not to fill them with food?"

Rachel did not know this, not that she thought it had anything to do with what she was dealing with. Comparing oranges to bananas annoyed her, and it showed on her face.

"You saw what almost happened on your last visit," Amy sternly reminded her. "Now, I suggest you talk with your Ethics Professor, and whatever you do, DO NOT do anything before FIRST talking with your friend. Now personally, if it were me," she added, pressing her chubby hand where that little silver slicker was probably still buried, "I would let her come to me. If she wants to talk with you, she will. If not, you need to leave it alone and let either her family or authorities deal with it."

Rachel did not like that spiel. She knew Michelle's mother, and her aunts. They were old fashioned women hellbent on setting her, and all women, back ages. And authorities weren't doing her friend any favors either. This was a prime case everyone needed to be swinging a bat at. Flustered she left Amy's office in tears, convinced she had to help Michelle on her own.

11...

If she was given a dollar for every quote referencing "not giving up," she could pay in cash the cost of tuition to attend Penn for four years. 'Keep moving'... 'failure is not an option'... 'quitters never win'... and one of the most obnoxious, 'don't stop'... probably a favorite of everyone with the name Amy, Kim, Joe, Julia, or had a vowel at the end of their name.

Like a soldier determined not to leave a comrade behind, she focused 110% on getting help for Michelle. First though, she had to cut off those who were part of the problem, thus Kim was the noise she sat on the curb first. Her negative energy burned a hole in her 'can-do' spirit. And Mrs. Perkins and the police, she put on her do not call list too. Josie and Amy's toxicity was unwelcomed as well. She didn't need them, even if she did take Amy's advice to get on Dr. Kirkland's calendar. The first day she sat in that ethics class she cringed for 45-minutes listening to a wishbone thin white woman lecturing on every issue but those pertaining to American women, while Michelle was suffering somewhere on U.S. soil. She gave up and left class early.

By the third lecture, her patience wearing thin, but determined to hang in there until the end of class she suffered through 2 hours of hearing about what was happening to women living in Ethiopia and Sudan and the darkest crevices of the globe. Female genitalia mutilations, harems, child brides and sex-slaves had never been a part of American culture but yet Dr. Kirkland felt these alien practices were necessary to commit to memory, even as many Arab and Muslim students objected throughout the lecture. "Some of these customs are practiced to teach obedience and respect," refuted one student. "Here in America there is too much freedom, no morality," he argued.

Then another student, from which country he came she did not know, stood and vehemently denounced the lecture too. "You Americans are weird. You believe in things which are not real. You think you are free, but you are slaves to ignorance and insanity, and your precious dollar bill. But you will see! You will see! Your gods have deceived you, for Allah is GREAT!" —And he stormed out of the room shouting again and again, Allah was great.

Many of the female students as well, native of countries around the globe, sat in silent defiance, shaking their head. Rachel didn't know exactly what about the lecture they objected to, because she was busy thinking about Michelle. That smile she lent her, for a brief timid second, was imprinted in her psyche. Despite how Kim felt, and what Amy said, and the professor holding firm to her teaching points being neither good or bad, right or wrong, there was a woman a few miles on the other side of the school suffering in silence.

"Look, research is research," Dr. Kirkland insisted. "I am only here to teach the legacy of practices—"

"—But why," interrupted a female student wearing jeans and a colorful head scarf. "How is this going to help us navigate from where we are today?"

Exactly!?! How was any of this discussion going to help 'bring Michelle home!?!'

But Dr. Kirkland held firm to her stance. "Having an understanding of cultural and religious practices from varying vantage points expands our worldview of—"

"—Not if it is propaganda," barked a student seated in the back of the lecture hall.

At this point Dr. Kirkland became frustrated, and notably disgusted. Her earlobe cut bob sitting on her head resembling a salt and pepper lamp shade, flopped around her face as she collected her teaching papers from the lectern. "Class is dismissed. We'll meet next Friday," she said with her head down.

More than a third of the class was out the door before she finished the last sentence. Rachel was among the few taking their time collecting their belongings, however she, with good reason. Patiently she waited for a student to finish speaking with the agitated professor. He was trying to get on her calendar too. Apparently, the only hours Dr. Kirkland had open was Sunday morning... or Saturday evening.

Obviously the woman had no family, or no life, or both. It was either that, or she found the perfect strategy to ensure only the most earnest students got her undivided attention. Rachel selected Sunday morning. For whatever it was worth, there was one aspect of the disputed research she 100% agreed with. For entirely too long men had been in control, exerting their opinions, beliefs and rules over women's minds and bodies.

But if she couldn't hear the omens howling, screaming she was headed in a wrongheaded direction, then she should've seen it Sunday morning when she looked around and saw the campus virtually deserted.

Generally, Sunday mornings was the most peaceful day of the week, likely anywhere, but certainly on campus. This was the day when students slept off gratifying weekends... and hangovers, procrastinating about preparing for a mundane Monday, when the aggravation would start all over again. But this Sunday seemed even more muted than the average. And not that she was usually up at this time on the holiest day of the week, she did expect at least a jogger ...or maybe a dogwalker to be out. But there was no one. It was so quiet and still out that she could hear the lanterns on 'The Walk' gossiping. Sounded like the buzzing was about her, one lantern asking another, 'now what is this fool up to, and where is she headed?'

She arrived at Marsha Kirkland's office, 8AM sharp. The room was surprisingly bright, and also shockingly empty. She would have thought a woman who wore bob hair-dos and talked about things that happened eons ago would spend much of her time in a den of clutter. But Marsha was organized. Neat as a pin and clean as a whistle.

"How are you doing today," the woman smiled, back nice and straight, as if she was in pain.

Rachel thought she muttered words to the equivalent of 'not well. I'm worried as hell and sleepy as hell along with it.' Yet what the professor heard was word vomit. Her butt barely touched the chair before she was rambling about her ride or die leaving Brown University—abruptly—in the middle of the first semester... acting different...likely resulting from being held hostage, probably being used as a sex-slave, definitely was being abused, and yet no one, absolutely no fucking one, was willing to step in and assist. For a solid speech-length five minutes she soiled a spotless clean office with what she knew about Michelle's situation, mentioning in conclusion how an adviser in the Student Affairs office confirmed her friend was living with a convicted murderer.

"Ump," Marsha hummed. "Now, which adviser is this?"

Stumped, Rachel thought for a second. What did Marsha Kirkland need with that information? What on earth good would it do to know the name of one adviser?

"I can't remember," she replied irritated. "Why?"

Admittedly her head was foggy. It was Sunday morning for crying out loud. She had been up since Friday reading about the habits and profiles of famous sex-traffickers, kidnappers and drug dealers, along with calling rape crisis interventionists and homeless shelters. After all, provided Mrs. Perkins stayed fixed to her rigid rules, and so long as her aunts and other relatives sided with the principles Julia subscribed to, Michelle was going to need a place to stay…of course, once her freedom was secured.

But it looked like the professor had grown a beard, and was sitting with her back facing Rachel when she finally stopped talking. Her face was gone. She saw no expression. There was a dark square in place of where a consoling advocate should've been. Between very tight teeth, which was all Rachel could see, Marsha snarled, "I teach Gender and Politics." And she said this putting a period on the end of her sentence. It was up to Rachel to pick up the ball and serve it back.

"But that's why I'm here," Rachel near pleaded. "Amy said you would help me…"

"Help you do what," Marsha replied so offended that the bob turned backwards looked lopsided.

"Help me get my friend away from a convicted murderer," Rachel shrieked.

"Why would I do that," Marsha snapped. "Do you understand that I—"

—Rachel didn't let her finish. She jumped up and woke the campus. "Because, BITCH, you advocate for women! You're supposed to be helping us! Not preaching about old shit no one knows about or wants to know about!"

The words tumbled out effortlessly, and of course sincerely. She hadn't slept in days. Her head hurt. She lost 20 pounds she couldn't afford to lose. When her mother left, years ago, she dropped the baby fat and hadn't been overweight since. At 5'7", 135 pounds was a decent size. 115 pounds was not. She looked like a hanger…with clothes thrown over it. She started to go for her wallet, to show Marsha what she used to look like, but didn't have a wallet on her.

Dr. Kirkland quietly watched the unglued Rachel for a while. Despite being yelled at, and called a bitch, she felt obligated to help her…if not only because she was a student, or a woman, but because she was a person.

"How are you doing in your classes," she gently asked.

Terrible was the answer. Fall semester she skated by. But Spring, she hadn't turned in one assignment because the only class she managed to attend, and stay awake in, was this class.

"Rachel, I need you to settle down and listen to me," Dr. Kirkland coolly said, instantly interrupting Rachel's labored breathing and manic pacing. "I want you to go back to your dorm and make a cup of tea, or whatever you need to relax," she continued, speaking in a voice that matched with the calm of a running dryer. "Then I want you to get a good night sleep, and Monday morning I want you back in class. I'll call after class with the information you'll need to help your friend."

Now. Was that so hard? It was all she wanted. Actually, the perfect pitch speaking volumes to not giving up, despite Dr. Kirkland's call not turning out as expected.

Speaking of volumes and cozy quotes, the upper echelon of the Penn community was more tightly knitted than she would have known to assume. From her level, the professors and associate professors seemed like a group of bobble heads pulled from a brainy-act sack. She had no idea, and for the longest would not appreciate the level of connectedness at the top.

Why would she expect anyone to know, much less remember her mother when she had forgotten her so many years ago? And not only did Dr. Kirkland find out about her mother, but she learned about Julia too. Little did she know, due to her cries, Michelle's story was floating all over the school, albeit in that small 10% academic top circle. This was nothing Rachel would've figured out, because she was still trying to figure out why she needed to speak with Julia.

"I want you to call Mrs. Perkins and set up a time to meet with her," Dr. Kirkland instructed. "…And I want you to be open to what she tells you, because it will not only help your friend, but affect your career."

Honestly, Rachel being clean out of options, couldn't dispute the professor, even if she wanted to. She pulled up in Julia's driveway and teared up the minute she did. The little red SUV was there, but not Michelle's dinged up Acura. Once upon a time she used to pull up behind Michelle's car and giggle, amused by her straddling the flower bed that used to so piss her mother off. Yeah, sometimes her friend could be so willful, and then she kind of had a right to be, given how her mother left her so little room to rebel.

Knocking at the door, a large white pronounced door that

said somebody meticulously clean owned the residence, brought on its own blend of anxiety. Truthfully, Rachel had been to the house hundreds, if not thousands of times, but the most she really knew about Mrs. Perkins was her last name. The rest she got from Michelle, which was downright unsettling...and unbelievable... but believable too. Like who doesn't cry at her husband's funeral? Even before Michelle's father's death, her mother was scary, speaking through digital tight lips imposing pointless rules like 'take off your shoes' and hair-brain curfews Michelle systematically ignored.

Mrs. Perkins opened the door and unlatched the glass storm door, and gently pushed it open to invite Rachel inside. First thing she noticed was how much older Mrs. Perkins looked. Before, when she was getting around on her broom, enjoying her position of bossing Michelle around and acting like nothing bothered her, it didn't look like the woman would ever age. Her skin was tight as her lips and taut as her eyes. A wrinkle existed nowhere. And she was always made up, no matter what time of day...or night. But not now.

"How have you been, Rachel?" Her voice sounded as fatigued as she looked, but so long as she didn't drink any of this woman's lemonade blindly, she just might spare herself from looking the same way. She was exhausted herself.

"Not well," she admitted. "I just miss her so much," she said barely above a whisper.

"We all do," Julia admitted as well. "Why don't you have a seat and let me take your coat," she replied as a matter of principle. She'd always been this way. Business first, even if she hadn't looked down at Rachel's feet like usual, not that she had to. Rachel knew the drill. She kicked off her shoes one step in the house.

"I...I...umm...I just want to apologize for—"

"—sssh, sssh, it's okay," Julia gently hushed her. "I couldn't call myself a mother if I hadn't gotten on you guys' nerves," she said, her voice dry as a bone, as if she'd been crying throughout Michelle's absence. "When you become a mother, you're going to be the same way. It's been this way for generations."

Rachel bowed her head and shrugged. Not that she agreed, but more so relieved she didn't have to relive how much of a tool they'd been too, acting the way they had, her and Michelle. Running over her flower bed and purposely tracking mud through the house at whatever hour theaters closed couldn't have been respectful...or nice. Michelle may have had a reason for being angry at her mother, but she couldn't help but recall their many mischievous deeds being so mean and unnecessary. If this woman was really like Michelle described, they would have been dead long before Mr. Perkins passed away.

"So, how's your dad?"

Rachel's head jolted up. Her dad? She didn't deal with him much. Secretly she often felt he devised that entire affair to run her mother away. After they divorced, he remarried, and a few years later remarried again. Now he was breaking down...dealing with early signs of MS. She didn't feel sorry for him one bit, made clear in her reply. "He moved to Florida," she said, a safety pin away from adding, 'with some whore,' when she heard Dr. Kirkland's voice. Truth was, the weather was supposedly better for his health. But rather than invite conversation about her father's karma she instead added, "we don't talk much as we used to."

"And your mother?"

Wow. She felt a headache coming. Here her daughter was in the hands of a murderer and she wanted to know how a petty thief was doing!?! "I haven't seen my mother in a while either," she quietly replied, balling her hands so tight she left nail prints in her palms. The question really hit low, recalling how Julia tried to sever her friendship with Michelle over her mother leaving, and now she cared? But Dr. Kirkland advised her to be professional, so she gritted her teeth and grinned.

"You know, I didn't always understand, or know why my mother said certain things or handled situations a particular way, but I always respected her," Julia said, her eyes cast down as she reflected on growing up, being so young and wanting to play with friends when her mother demanded she look after her younger siblings. Only the girls were made to work inside the home, while boys were allowed to carouse in the streets, after the heavy lifting chores albeit. For the longest she wished she were born a boy, and too, she also wished her mother hadn't had so many children. It was a while before she understood that time period, and the challenges her mother faced and solved on limited resources.

"I realize now I gave Wren the rope she is now using to strangle herself," Julia continued. "For some reason I was convinced if she didn't have to struggle, she'd make better decisions. I completely misjudged the value in some struggles and sacrifice. I think we all did."

That was Rachel's cue to let Mrs. Perkins know she wasn't talking into dead space. "I'm learning that now," she piped in. "I'm failing almost all of my classes, but the sacrifice to help Shelly is way more important than my superficial needs."

Julia looked at Rachel, like most people looked at a running tap waiting for the water to warm up. Blank-faced. "Oh child," she sighed. "Don't throw your education away for Wren," she said. "She's not thinking about either you or I. I saw her a few days ago.

She's perfectly fine. They're making plans to get married in the Bahamas, once the baby is born. Has she sent you an invitation?"

That did it. Indeed she was hurt. Very hurt. Kicked down, knocked out, hurt. They had made a pack to be the maid or matron of honor at each other's weddings. They also would be godparent to each other's children. So far Michelle had broken every one of their bonds. It was like a 10-year marriage, no warning, suddenly ending... and not ending after a fiery crash on 76, or due to a terminal illness, but due to a deceitful friend that had never been a friend in the first place.

She cried in her pillow many nights, and brought sewing pins to stick in sock puppets she turned into voodoo dolls to sic on Michelle. She cursed her, and cursed her child, hoping nothing but the worst for who she began referring to as her ex. She even started hating the name Michelle.

That was her wake up call. The kick in the pants that got her head in the right game. Along with the help of counselors and communities within Penn, and of course Dr. Kirkland and even Amy, she returned to her studies and career. She had to work hard to get off academic probation, but within months she made other friends, connected with professors, and worked in the community to organize food and clothing drives, along with leading computer workshops for women seeking to enter the workforce. She also accepted an internship at a media company, Brand Voices, which put her on the path to do what she wanted to do since she was a little girl. Write a book… and hopefully of course, a best-selling book.

And yet, the work she cherished most, what cushioned her comeback, was volunteering for the House of Purpose Evangelists. HOPE was a community group who served women, mothers and their children in abusive relationships. They not only housed, and fed and clothed struggling families, but they provided them with tools to live better lives. Rachel loved the work because not only was she helping people in their greatest time of need, but these people got her through some dark days as well.

While she ran around collecting clothes and shoes and furnishings, networking with groups and churches and individuals to help secure employment for some of the ladies, the women in return taught her valuable life lessons. 'Don't believe everything you hear'. 'Check your sources.' And most important, 'hard as it may be to accept, you can't help nobody that don't want to be helped.'

No one more so than Nina Warren taught her this lesson, an excruciatingly hard way. Nina was a petite, very pretty girl, only 19, with 3 children. Two little girls, Sierra and Zianica, one and two; and 6-month-old Cai. Nina came to HOPE with a black-eye and chipped tooth, begging counselors to help her. For several months she'd been dating an insanely jealous 57-year-old man; and who could blame a broke porter who moved out of his mother's basement after spending five years incarcerated and living a year on the street. He fell in love with this girl who thought she could rescue him, and show him the beauty in living a decent life. She had built an event planning business, had clients, some well-known, and her bank statements proved she could afford her own place, where he in fact moved into… and a month later wouldn't leave. She was trying to get away from him, and had come to HOPE mostly for protection. She just needed a place to lay low until her flight departed. But the shelter didn't have the best accommodations, plus she was concerned about someone recognizing her and informing her abuser. So Carole Porter, a 69-year-old grandmother, volunteered to offer Nina and her children a bedroom in her home. After all, Nina was an ideal client. Someone who made a few mistakes, but worked hard and wasn't looking for a handout. The five of them left that Friday, and except for their funeral, no one ever saw them again.

A shock to everyone at HOPE, many were aghast that it was Nina who called her abuser, despite being so frightened that she didn't want to stay in the shelter. She had been willing to spend all of her money relocating clear across the country, at the added expense of having to start all over, and yet she gave the guy Carole's address so he could say goodbye to his son. Just tragic, and incomprehensible.

And yet, many women living in shelters did this all the time. But in many cases, it was somewhat understandable. The women were desperate; often in need of financial support, and sometimes even physical reprieve. But Nina was one of a rare few who didn't need that guy for nothing. Rachel could not get over the tragedy. Carole was a beautiful woman too; and not that the children…and even Nina deserved their fate, because they didn't. Just so senseless. And to make matters worse, the guy was about to kill himself… until Nina called. Just WoW. Horrible.

If it weren't for the trust these women placed in her, confiding many things meant to be taken to graves, along with the disclosure affidavit she signed, she would've written that book, while still at Penn, about the hundreds of incidents she encountered working for HOPE.

Four years she worked with HOPE before graduating… and on time with honors. She left Penn…and HOPE…with a bevy of experiences about people, and relationships and the conditions of being human. Kim and her kids attended the commencement activities. Their parents did not. But it didn't matter. It was a gorgeous day and an exhilarating moment. After the ceremonies, and on her dime, Kim took her and her children to a popular seafood grill downtown. They ate and talked and caught up for hours. She had finally been promoted, working as a senior budget coordinator in the finance department at the school board. That became the joke of the evening; Kim with her hands on numbers and money, after the shame their mother caused the school board. All the same, things were looking up for her and she was happy. She sold her old home, bought a new one, plus a brand-new car, and had spare change to buy Rachel a brand-new car too.

"I can't take this," Rachel told Kim. "You still have Roger and Brit to get through college…"

"…Just take the damn car and say thank you," Kim sighed. During their make-up exchanges she already told her baby sister she felt bad about her getting such a raw deal. Between their mother leaving, or getting kicked out, whichever version was more handy at the time of its mention, and their father letting Rachel raise herself, she basically had been deserted. It wasn't fair and Kim regretted she didn't see it at the time.

But Rachel had her regrets too. She should've never kicked her sister to the curb, like Kelly…their other sister…had done them. Kelly was a senior at Penn State when their parents were going through their ordeal. After she graduated, she flew to San Francisco and never looked back. They hadn't heard from her since. Wouldn't know what she looked like. Didn't know if she was dead or alive, which often pained Rachel thinking she could have lost Kim, the only family she really had, the same way had she left her at the curb.

"Well, you might've thought you had kicked me to the curb, but I had eyes on you the whole time," Kim teased. And she had. She knew a few people who worked at Penn. One of them being the 'ole gun-slinging Amy, another big laugh.

Jokes aside, Kim couldn't have been prouder of her baby sister, watching 'the Rock' pull her big girl panties up and lace up her boots to get through school. "You're always looking out for others," she added. "For a change let me do something for you."

That was a major statement, though Rachel knew this was only partially true. Had it not been for so many hands and hearts; Joe, Amy, Dr. Kirkland and even Mrs. Perkins and definitely her big sister Kim, there was no telling where'd she be. Deep inside she knew her journey had yet to begin. As hard as she tried to forget her ex, and the many times she stuck pins in that sock puppet hoping Michelle felt each poke, she felt the sting. So she threw the puppet away hoping to God wherever Michelle was, she was okay.

And then it happened. Several months after graduating she happened to be in Fresh Grocer at 40th and Walnut picking up balloons and a bon voyage card for a colleague when she ran into Michelle. Theoretically, everything that happened that afternoon wasn't supposed to happen. Rarely did she get out to West Philly. She, in fact, hadn't been back since graduating. But she had contacted an old professor about a possible job opportunity. Not that she didn't like where she was, but she didn't want to be like her sister, letting a year turn into a decade and she still be proofing stories and volunteered to pick up balloons for colleagues moving on to greener pastures.

So, there she was, short on time trying to kill two birds with one stone when she spotted this woman and two little boys looking in the refrigerator where she was headed. Soon as she spotted them, the woman with her big booty holding open the refrigerator door, and the little boys pointing, she prayed they would hurry up and get what they wanted. The office farewell bon voyage started at noon and it was 11:39 when she hopped out of the car. That gave her 21 minutes to grab a 9x12 sheet cake, check out and drive up Walnut and over Lancaster without getting stopped by police. Fat chance. A momma with a behind that big had nothing to do but hold everybody else up.

Sure enough, the woman who had her back turned when she reached the fridge, also had another little one in the shopping cart, which also blocked access to the sheet cakes.

"But T, mommy can buy some chocolate ice-cream," the woman explained to the taller child with the large golden locks. "Everybody might not want all chocolate cake..."

At that moment, as the mother was trying to reason with the child, Rachel caught sight of her profile. The woman looked like Michelle Renee Perkins. Heavier, but the same features; bubbly lips, tiny bubble nose, and the identical flat forehead and brown complexion. "Shelly," she whispered.

Michelle turned around. Indeed it was her. "Rocky," she shrieked, when a flicker of their last encounter looked like it darted across her face. She hesitated for a second, splitting that moment to pull one child out of the freezer before the door closed on him.

"Oh my God Rocky!" she squealed. "Where have you been!?! I haven't seen you in a minute!"

Two out-stretched arms and two-inch navy painted nails came at her, pulling her into an embrace she did not reciprocate. For some reason her arms refused to respond. But Michelle didn't seem to notice as she stepped back.

"Look at you," she beamed. "Still got that pretty hair!"

Michelle always had pretty hair too, but speaking of "look at her," she looked at her ex-bestie. She had really filled out. All boobs and booty. She no longer looked like the naïve suburban girl, but had turned into one of them SWV sex pot chicks they used to idolize. And going back to the hair thing, Michelle had cut hers off. She wore it like Piggy Grier on the 'Steve Harvey' sitcom. In other words, her hair was slaying.

"These are my kids," she went on, oblivious to the hell her ex-bestie suffered trying to endure their break-up. "This is my oldest, Teton," she smiled with the glossy whites and burgundy wet lips. "...And this is my little guy Ryker, and my boo Marcellus," she added so full of pride Rachel's upper lip hiked up an inch.

It wasn't that she didn't like kids or that the children weren't 100% adorable to look at. The three little faces she saw were too precious to ignore. The oldest had stunningly blue eyes and curly golden-brown hair. The other little guy was a chocolate cutie with huge brown eyes and strikingly coal black straight hair. Even the baby in the buggy was a sweetie, but in a way most chubby 8-month-old pink, green-eyed babies with no hair were sweet.

What bothered Rachel was Michelle's beam, her inflated happiness and buttery brown complexion. She looked so healthy, and definitely well-fed, but was blind as a bat if she could not see the hurt on her face.

"Well, I'm sure you have your hands full," Rachel said, eager to back her way out of this exchange. And it wasn't because the minutes were ticking. She had forgotten all about the noon bon voyage. Those 21 minutes she had to get across West Philly to City Avenue had dwindled down to ten. The cake definitely was going to be late.

"Guurl!" Michelle playfully huffed, stomping her foot.

"These kids be working my nerves sometimes...do you have any?" Rachel stared at the woman glittering and glowing in front of her, as if trying to figure out where they met. She remembered the Michelle she met in 2nd grade, and thought it was her. She had the same brown skin and smiley eyes and deep dimples. The bubble lips definitely looked the same. They were especially memorable because Michelle used to pout a lot. And when she got the braces, her bubbly lips were even more pronounced. Excise the street jargon and she was positive it was the same person, yet she replied like she would to a stranger.

"No, I prefer to borrow them," she joked, patting Michelle on the shoulder like doctors with great bedside manners patted patients.

"Oh, hey..." Michelle called after her. "Lemme get your number..."

Mid-motion, headed towards express checkout, with Michelle and her darlings a few feet behind her, she stopped...and froze. Had she heard right? Did this heffa have the unmitigated gall to ask for her phone number? Was she high, or drunk? Because she looked pretty sober. It was then when it dawned on Rachel. Perhaps that person really wasn't Michelle. Maybe she had been thinking so hard about Michelle that she just imagined it was her.

Slowly, like done in movies, she turned around, this time taking particular care to study the woman. Funny. On first inspection she mistook the glitz and flashing bling for glass. It was not. Upon closer inspection those were diamonds on her fingers and around her wrist. Real diamonds. Her eye went straight to the Tiffany bracelet, a piece of jewelry she'd spot anywhere. This particular bracelet was from the Garland collection, which had a dated feminine look, a contrast to the bulky (more masculine) Buccellati band on her finger. A closer looked revealed the leaf patterns in both, just stunning as a set. She almost got trapped in all that glass. The other things jingling on her might not have been as expensive, but those who wore authentic jewelry didn't sully up real with fake. Head to toe Michelle rocked the best. Even the little boys were wearing Jordans, leading to another wonder. Who did she know!?!

"So, what'chew doing out here," she laughed as the blue nails tapped the phone.

The better question was why was she in public begging to be robbed!?! Not that it was any of her business but Rachel told her she was visiting her school, and had stopped in the store to pick up a cake for a colleague who was leaving the company.

"Oh, that's right... you still at Penn, huh?"

"No, I graduated this summer," she replied.

Michelle didn't respond. She was concentrating on finding the app to plug in her phone number. "Well guuurl, I got this new phone," she said, frowning at her gold iPhone trying to make it do what she wanted it to do. "...I think I liked my Samsung better," she casually added, acting as if their running into each other was a happy accident.

Rachel just watched her, feeling her legacy flip-phone buzzing in her purse. Someone at the office was probably calling, wondering where she was.

"All right, now give me your number," Michelle finally said, holding the phone with one hand and reaching for her boys playing hide-n-seek around her legs.

Rachel smiled, not at the boys, but about a memory Kim shared when a guy she didn't care for 'asked for her digits'. She gave the guy a bogus number, like no sweat, she dodged a creep, except the creep having been through this rigamarole called the number while she was standing there holding the phone. Busted. Why Rachel didn't attempt the same trick.

Later she would replay the events of this chance meeting, how the karma that separated them, put them in the same place at the same time. Of course, she didn't know any of this then. She only thought about getting a new phone and changing her number.

She returned to work and bumped into Liz, a graduate of Villanova who was among the cluster of interns offered permanent fulltime employment at the same time as she. From day one they synced. Unlike the bond she had with Michelle, theirs was more natural. None of the fake liking the same things, or both hating their mothers and subscribing to unwritten rules. They were however, both born under the same Zodiac sign—the bull, and products of a mixed marriage. Liz's father was black, and mother Irish. And Rachel's parents had just the opposite composition. Her father was Irish and mother black. Both sets of parents however, were divorced. And their daughters, both communication majors, were passionate reading and writing advocates.

    "Girl, it looks like you've seen a ghost," Liz laughed, the both of them standing in the office kitchen alone. "Don't worry, nobody liked that old fart anyway." She was talking about Ed, a 55-year-old who rolled into Voices when the company was in Germantown printing newsletters on gifted ink jet printers and distributing them by hand. Contributorily, Liz thought Rachel was concerned about returning with the cake and card a little late. Many were back at their desk with plates of Swedish meatballs, chicken walnut salad and slices of green apples by the time she got back.

    But Rachel had already spoken to their direct boss Angie Wilkerson. She told her to slow down too. "Just pass the card around for everyone to sign and make sure Ed gets it before he leaves," she instructed. She was much too busy, with far greater concerns than to be shaking up one day over one person about to leave the company anyway.

    "I actually think I did see a ghost," Rachel replied to Liz, sighing in a daze. "I just saw my ex..."

    "Your ex," shrieked Liz. "I didn't know we were dating!"

"We aren't...and it's not that kind of ex," Rachel snapped, snatching a paper towel from the dispenser to vigorously wipe cake residue off her fingers.

But Liz wasn't paying the attitude much attention. She was holding the cake box lid open, smiling at what was inside. "Ugh... Rache, you might want to be a little more necromantic, and less primordial in your messaging," she giggled.

Rachel spun around, confused by Liz's epistle. But a quick glance told her what she kind of expected. Liz was making fun of the cake. A huge Minion eyeball attached to a speak bubble talking about "see ya' later" wasn't the greatest choice for an adult leaving the company to go make money for someone else. But hey, she was in a hurry.

"Well, you should've seen what I had to reach over," she wryly chuckled, still worked up about seeing her ex. "...I could've grabbed one of the cakes with the baby paw smears, or maybe made one of my own," she bitterly scoffed.

"Oh, so you bake too?" Liz asked surprised, ignoring the other part of her scoffing. Rachel wouldn't strike the average person as someone who spent much time in a kitchen. She was razor thin, pretty, and never came to work with a chipped nail. But Liz started detecting an abnormal despondency about her. "Are you okay? Is it the ex thing?"

"Actually it is," Rachel admitted. "What would you do if you ran into someone who you were really close to, and for no reason they suddenly stopped speaking and totally went ghost?"

"Aaah," Liz stalled to think a minute. "I don't know," she admitted too. Like Rachel she didn't talk about guys and dating. Making Associate Editor, traveling the globe and writing books consumed most of their idle chatter when they weren't talking about a hot story, or the two hottest women in the company, Regina A. Palmer and Wendy E. Wooten.

"I probably should've just flat asked what her problem was," Rachel said disgusted, and not at Michelle, but with herself. While her ex braggingly introduced her kids and teetered about nothing, flashing real glass in her face and acting as if nothing had happened, she stood there hurting inside, trying to figure out what she really was feeling. In the car, on the way back to work, she decided it probably was jealousy. That's why she didn't react, or say anything at the primal time, the moment when all she had to do was just ask. But that's how it typically went 'in the heat of a moment.'

By the end of the week, after telling Liz how Michelle almost stole four years of her life, without apology, between assignments they started surfing the Internet to see if Michelle was active online. Really, they had no central theme as to what they were look-ing for, surprise being the beast at the core of every good story. Twitter, Facebook and the dating sites... Match.com, Tinder and PlentyofFish, along with the White Pages were key targets. They skipped LinkedIn, and Goodreads too, since it never entered their mind that women who wore the kind of jewelry Rachel described either worked or read. "Maybe you should see if that woman is still at Penn," Liz suggested at one point. "I bet she knows more than what she showed you."

Rachel disagreed, but didn't disclose why, not that it had any bearing on their search. She could always tap her sister for Amy's whereabouts if she really needed to. Plus, there was always Michelle's mother, Mrs. Perkins, who for sure could tell her more, and a lot quicker than a ratchet algorithm.

By the end of the week she started getting bored with the fruitless search. She didn't even know Michelle's new last name, and found herself drifting into other people's lives and business that had nothing to do with Michelle, work or the countless other random things she cared about. Finally, late one afternoon, after about a month or so of the half-hearted 'searching for Michelle', she told Liz, "...you know what, I'm done. I think I'm healed."

This announcement was a problem for Liz. Their careers revolved around research and getting a story. This was the mood that enveloped the environment they marinated in 8, 9, and on oc-casions 10 or more hours a day. Their brains were hotwired to turn-ing so much as an untied shoelace into a leading story. There was no way Liz could sit on those huge glass rocks Rachel described and say or do nothing, and she told Rachel so. "There's no way we can, or should let this one go," she argued, at first politely. "Do you know what this can do for our careers? Plus, there's a good chance your friend still needs help," she added. "I bet she doesn't even know she's living with a convicted murderer."

But Rachel was not there with Liz, and for one main rea-son. Michelle used to be her friend. There was a difference be-tween spreading rumors about someone who hurt her feelings and presenting those rumors as fact in hard cold print for the world to read...and archive. So Rachel dug her heels in, and it pissed Liz off. She had spent all those weeks investing not only her time, but emo-tions on this story. Cat essentially out of the bag she was not drop-ping the story and thought Rachel was crazy for carrying a torch for someone who ghosted her.

"Look, even if my ex deserves to be called out, I will have to live with my conscience," she told Liz whose jaws grew tight.

"Oh, it's cool," Liz snapped. "I didn't come here to make

friends anyway. I came here to make money!"

"Well then, I definitely wouldn't waste my time on that... unless you're trying to move over to FPN," Rachel teased.

It was a joke, even if what wasn't so funny was the health of FPN. Of the four divisions in the company, Front Page News (or FPN) was the online editorial arm to Brand Voices, which according to bottom line reports shared in staff meetings, its profit margins were the weakest in the company. The two head bosses, tough and frightening as they took unlimited pleasure in portraying themselves to be, still hadn't figured out how to get paying subscribers for their online content. No one wanted to have anything to do with FPN. No one but those on probation for disciplinary reasons, along with entry-level editors Voices was taking a chance on. Word in the building was anyone assigned to that division was on his or her last leg, on their way out if they couldn't show results.

Liz turned up her nose as if something smelled in the room. "Oh no sugar plums, we're going to see who's going to end up on Front Page News!"

Sure enough, a few days later Rachel and Angie got into a big confrontation. It started when as Angie passed by her cubicle something on her screen caught her attention, making her take a foxtrot step back. "What are you working on," she had asked, to which Rachel replied, "a story I'm trying to fact check." It wasn't the truth. She was commenting on a blog about the big debate over e-Books versus physical books. But so what! Every day she walked by workstations and saw website pages on computer screens that had nothing to do with work. Printed Amazon purchase receipts littered the printer area. And she was constantly shredding and tossing forgotten copies of illicit and very explicit material left on the fax machines and copiers. But the real animus was, she really had thought about submitting a column on the whole e-Book/real book debate. She didn't have to downsize or defend a thing.

Angie, however, didn't like her tone, or maybe she really didn't like her. She told her to lower her voice, and Rachel clapped back, telling her to lower hers. "Look, I distribute the hours around here," Angie rowed. And Rachel yelled back, "well, I don't recall your name on the bottom of any of my checks!"

That did it. Angie wrote her up for insubordination and laid the violation on her desk, with big red (all caps) letters printed boldly across the top...FINAL WARNING!

Rachel flew into a rage, which just so happened, an event that had the likelihood of a one in 10,000th chance of ever happening, Wendy strutted by. Rachel never saw her as she shouted Angie was full of shit. And she had no back-up plan in the pipeline. The job announcement she went to see about at Penn wasn't a fit. She wasn't interested in becoming Toni Morrison's clone, working as someone's assistant to get a book deal. So for her to come out blindly swinging, as if she was about to become her sister's clone, languishing for decades letting a company screw her around, was some kind of chiffonade karma.

As soon as she saw the vice-president round the corner headed to her office, a woman who rarely made appearances and everyone talked about as if they were speaking of God, promenaded it was lights out for her.

She didn't keep trinkets on her desk, so there was no need to run around looking for boxes, yet expecting guards to show up she started cleaning her laptop for files she wanted to keep. Her only consolation at the moment was that Liz wasn't in the studio seeing any of this. Actually, no one was around, which partly contributed to why she did what she did at the time she did. She could have easily defended herself because she likely would be using the best alibi of all times; "I wasn't yelling," "...I never said that,"... "they're just taking her side,"...and yada, yada, yada... 'my word against hers', which she would have been telling HR, and not the Shero herself, who indeed wanted to see her, in her office; the message delivered by a happy Angie wearing a pleasant smirk.

Both knees shaking so hard she could hear them knocking, she vibrated down the hallway reminded she was about to come face-to-face with a woman so very few did.

Wendy Eleanor Wooten came with the furniture and first coat of paint, way back in the late 80's when her and Michelle were swapping blood. She joined her cousin Regina Palmer, the founder and president of Brand Voices, to embark on a two-woman show in Regina's parent's three-story ramshackle building on the cobbly part of Germantown Avenue in Maplewood Mall.

Brand Voices was hardly an overnight success however. Far from it, why the women were viewed like monuments. They spent almost 11 years printing community newsletters on a copier gifted to them by a cousin who was the principal at Pickett Middle School. Only able to print enough papers to reach 2500 homes, they collected enough 'feel-good community stories' that their little two-woman show caught the attention of a media mogul.

Ross Bell bought stake in the company's philanthropy... and news spreading like wild fire around the city, and brought them up the corporate ladder to City Ave, under the umbrella of Tri-State TV. From there marked their true rise. Within years apart the sheroes, featured among Who's Who, were running a newspaper circulating across the nation, and talked about world-wide. They also printed two magazines and had a plug on PBS radio, along with their latest online endeavor still in its sink or swim phase. In every sense of the phrase Wendy and Gina (as she was called) were true movers and shakers. Everyone who worked for them, wanted to be in their good graces...and too...one day in their shoes.

She entered Wendy's office humbled. After many months as a fulltime Voice, and so many years interning, she finally landed on the vice-president's radar...for the worst possible reason.

"What was that I heard out there," Wendy pointedly asked, opening and closing drawers and doing other busy work while waiting on a response.

"...But you didn't hear everything," she began, her voice cracking some. "All day, every day Angie ignores what's going on out there, but picks on those who just started, or who she doesn't like," and she continued on, recounting in a rambling fashion the many violations she witnessed on the daily.

"So, what are you working on," Wendy curtly interrupted. She stammered, and then outright lied, trying to paint a clear image of the real villain and victims. She really didn't have to do this though. Not only was fact-checking in the course of the work editors did, an illusive foible to prove or disprove, Angie was far out of bounds digging into her the way she had. But she was nervous. She'd never met this woman up close and so personal before, barely spoke to her, only knowing of her from the Brand Voices' story... and gossip.

So, shaken, she lied, bumbling through a half-baked story about Michelle planning to kill her mother, and her wanting to spare young people from a similar fate. The story made no sense, and coalesced in no way, shape, form or fashion whatsoever with what was going on in the book world. Had Wendy grilled her on this lie, she and her entire saga would have fallen apart on the spot. Except Wendy liked the story. "I want you to finish that story and bring it to me...only me," she stressed. "Front Page News might be able to use a story like that."

16...

She couldn't remember what Wendy wore, much less what she really looked like, or even what they talked about, but Liz's abrupt change carved gullies so deep in her cranium that she could spend the rest of her life seeing therapist after therapist. The one or two snippy word exchanges turned into complete avoidance. It was painful, in many ways far worse than the trauma Michelle inflicted on her because, unlike Michelle, she confided in Liz, pouring out her heart explaining what it felt like being ghosted. And making matters worse, Liz turned the screw when she ponied up with a woman who didn't seem to have a friend in the world. No one to help her dress. No one to assist with styling her hair, and definitely no one to tell her, her unsolicited advice was not welcome. They (her and Liz) used to gossip about this editor daily, what made this slap in the face really sting. The only solace was the fact that no one in the studio had ever told an executive where the sun wasn't shining in front of a living legend and received a full pardon, and 'sort of like' promotion...even if this lifeline thrown her way went nowhere near breaking any tapes.

And then one day, Liz was gone. It was like one minute she was there, and a bathroom break later her side of the cubicle was completely cleaned out. The calendar she kept pinned to the partition wall, a visual reminder of staff meetings, and the old linty sweater she kept hung on her chair to let roving employees know the seat was taken had all disappeared. Even the docking station was gone, as if someone deliberately wanted to emphasize her sudden absence.

It was in this altered exodus, feeling for normalcy, such as a place to plant her feet, unsure who she reported to, whether Wendy, Angie or someone else, and unable to determine who next to confide in or trust, that she pulled out her phone. She opened her contacts, about to reach out to her alma mater, when she smelled cologne—a soft Chanel scent, and felt a presence in the same instance she heard her voice. "So, have you finished the story we spoke about," Wendy asked like state troopers crept up on speeding motorists. One minute the coast was clear. A second later flashing lights and a tap on the window.

She thought a moment, fighting her way out of the mental fog, wondering what was going on. Where was Liz? And why was she feeling like she'd been stranded on an island...with Wendy? Naturally she stammered. "I wasn't sure how to submit the essay. I keep hearing how hard it is to get on your calendar..."

Wasn't no lie there. Wendy rarely being in the office, along with a watch dog guarding her calendar, was all the proof a jury needed. Still, Wendy's eyes narrowed and glowered, and her lips parted, though no words came out. She took a minute to think too. "Well, I was hoping when I had dinner with my friend tonight, I would have something to give her," she said standing over her with the same purpose of the state trooper waiting for a license to appear, that didn't exist.

"...I think I have a copy on one of my flash drives," she said swallowing hard. She had hundreds of stories on memory sticks. She had been keeping a diary since meeting Michelle. Old looseleaf notebooks she misplaced when her father ran off with his new wife, but when she got to Penn, she started storing her precious thoughts on flash drives she hoped, at least one, preferably the latest, was in her purse. It was almost 3PM, a couple of hours before the normal 'end of the day'. It would take that long to drive home and return, and that was provided there was zero traffic and she got all greens.

"Good," Wendy replied. "Because Liz showed Gina a book outline that blew her mind." ...And though Liz's workstation was as clean as a kitchen that had never been used, she leaned over and whispered in her ear anyway. "She's giving her a month to work from home to write it."

After Wendy strutted off, hoisting her Louboutin hobo bag over her shoulder like she threw her synthetic full lace ketwig behind her, Rachel dove into her little Fossil purse. She dug in it like a squirrel in a batch of leaves fishing for nuts. She got to sweating...and panting, fearing it might be stuck in her desktop at home. "It's gotta be here," she muttered to herself, turning the purse upside down and viciously shaking the contents on her desk. It would be terrible karma, after taking great pleasure in telling her boss she was full of shit and not losing her job, all to miss out on an opportunity of a lifetime. It wasn't funny, and then again it was, but even heathens knew how to pray. Somehow, someway shewas taking

Wendy up on this godsend offer to work from home doing the one thing she longed to do. Write a book!

Soon as she spotted the memory stick, she popped that baby in her laptop, without it ever dawning on her; "this all might be too good to be true." All in her head was, whatever bizarre game Wendy and Gina had going on, they were about to lose because she was ready to play.

Tiz the season she selected the folder '2009' and the file 'WSW', Women Supporting Women. Like she expressed in her interview, she had been an active follower of Brand Voices' core values, long before she arrived at the company. Call her Miss Mission Accomplished. A front-running powerful woman who wore the boss emblem like a purple-heart warrior was in for a special treat. Everything Brand Voices stood for was embroidered in this essay; suspense, intrigue, compassion and passion, plus the overall message was deep...and genuine. The grit it took to help a friend she suspected of being held against her will by a convicted murderer was real talk.

But Wendy hardly fell backwards. "What is this I'm reading," she asked big-eyed, holding in her hand what she viewed as a self-indulgent trials and tribulations tear fest.

Did this child not realize she had taken a two-woman show all the way to the third floor of a building owned by Comcast. They now occupied three floors of that building, employing over 10,000 people, which included stay-at-home moms, retired grandmoms, and anyone willing to share heartfelt personal stories in one of their 'Dear Editor' columns. Brand Voices was the face of storytelling, inspiring individuals worldwide, from incarcerated men and women...all the way up to dignitaries leading nations. So little Miss Mission Accomplished Wannabe Purple Heart Warrior, sitting in a cubicle she paid rent on, had to come with more than a tired 'Dear Abby' sounding column.

Rachel read her tone instantly, and was heartbroken to hear "that mess" was unsuitable to show her friend. "I can't show this train-wreck to anyone," Wendy heaved.

"Look," she continued, sighing exasperated. "I'ma need you to take this email I'm about to send you, home. I want you to sit down and carefully go over those questions, and then get back to me with the answers. I'm still giving you a month! But I'm looking for something substantial... something like what Liz handed Gina!"

Click!

She wasn't a religious person, going to church every Sunday believing in spirits and gods and whatnot. She likely wasn't even a spiritual person. Excluding the forgotten years when her mother dressed her up for Easter, her coincidental run-ins with religion and church simmered down to attending weddings and funerals. That was about as spiritually grounded as it got for her. But she did believe in luck and the other 'L' word. Logic.

Had Michelle not asked for her number, and more so, had she not obliged the gesture plugging Michelle's number into her phone, she would've needed far more than a month using her imagination to respond to Wendy's questionnaire. Only someone who had been there and through it could fill in those gaping holes.

Karma refusing to move along, Michelle answered her call on the first ring. "Hey chica! I've been meaning to call you," she clamored. "Guuurl, we've got to meet up and talk," she said in this big burst of energy, as if she was on to Wendy and Gina too. "You busy this weekend?"

Rachel hardly needed to access a calendar. She was making dinner reservations while Michelle ran her mouth. "Have you ever heard of Devons?"

"Devons? Naw girl, never heard about that one," Michelle replied. "Is it out there on the Main Line? I don't get over there much..."

"No. It's a seafood grill, downtown... I'll text you the address," she shot off, her fingers mowing over a keyboard faster than lightning struck ground. The call lasted less than a minute. Twenty-six seconds to be exact; most of that time spent typing in the reservation. She had hang-up calls last longer. The call went so well she doubted Michelle would show. Except, karma doing what caught the attention of so many, Michelle did show up. In fact, she got there first. The hostess pointed her out, sitting at the bar tapping on her phone with her back facing the door.

She spun around and her face lit up the moment she realized Rachel had arrived. "Hey guuurl," she chirped, hopping off the stool and embracing her the same way she had in the grocery store. "I'm hungry. I sure hope the food here is good!"

"Oh, don't worry. It is," Rachel replied, more business-like than friendly. This definitely was not the same girl she had grown up with, the Shelly who sulked and pouted and wore braces over her huge teeth making her lips look bigger and poutier. That girl was gone, but was the same hip-hop sexy cute looking woman she bumped into in Fresh Grocer.

They sat down and Michelle immediately got to looking around. "It's nice in here," she remarked. "I'm surprised Vin ain't bring me here before."

Rachel smiled...and watched her, part amused, part envious, but mostly disgusted. As much as she wanted to hate her for her fake friendship, acting like their bond meant nothing, she hated herself more for basking in this sick game. "I always come here. I love the crabcakes and service," she coolly replied, noticing that her fake ex wasn't wearing nearly as much jewelry as before. 'Hummp, probably was borrowed...or better...repossessed' she ruefully beamed inside.

"I know that's right! I love me some crabcakes," Michelle piped in, loud and brassy as she picked up the menu to run her eyes up and down the list before carefully turning the page with those long wild nails. This time they were painted cranberry. Probably to blend with the huge gold butterfly ring on her thumb.

Unbelievable. She could not get over how this fly chick paraded her new, showing no sign of remorse. She didn't even attempt to apologize for how that man treated her; kicking her out of his house the way he did, almost breaking her sister's car window, and acting like he wouldn't lose a night's sleep if he had killed them both. It was surreal, so she continued watching her, albeit when her eyes were in the menu, or scanning the room trying to see what was on other diners' plates. While she dressed the part, she hardly was as affluent as the artillery she hid behind. Those who could afford the labels she dressed in, didn't scream across half the dining room about the cost of a $29.99 dish. Reminded her of the hood rats she sat beside in classes at Penn, plagiarizers who could recite the credits of Lord Dudley or King Edward the 3rd, but didn't know the name of their grandfather who washed Wanamaker's windows.

"Oool Gurl! I wonder if this lobster tastes like the picture..." Michelle squealed, her eyes pulsating at the pretty images, and narrowing when she saw something she didn't recognize.

"...Umm, I'm trying to figure out why you ghosted me," Rachel asked pointedly, pointing out the real elephant in the room, nothing that ventured near the topics she needed to cover.

Michelle looked across the table and let her eyes drop beneath the menu. "Girl, you wouldn't understand the half of it," she sighed.

"Try me." Rachel was not playing around. She was there, strictly on business. None of what happened was funny to her.

And so Michelle did, breezing over how she had gotten into trouble at Brown and was trying to fix her life before she, or anyone else found out what really went down. "You know how my mother is...I just didn't want to hear it."

"...And so you ghosted me," Rachel shrugged annoyed. "I thought—"

"—Damnit Rocky! It wasn't all about you," she quietly huffed, using this moment to move silverware aside so she could pick up the dinner napkin, shake it open and spread across her lap. "Actually, maybe if you had cared more about us, than just you, we wouldn't have to go back that far," she giggled.

What!?! That was the expression Rachel gave Michelle. "Do you realize I—" —and she quickly dialed back the anger. "All you had to do was say something ...Instead of—"

"—Instead of what Rocky," she snapped. "Instead of taking care of my issues so that I didn't disrupt your happiness?!"

At that moment the waiter returned to the table to take their orders. Michelle wanted the fried calamari for starters, and one of the high-roller cocktails. "And oh, I'm taking care of this..." she slung across the table.

"...Except for Elvis, I'll have the same," Rachel joked with the waiter looking down at them smirking. "You know what," she said leaning over her plate soon as the waiter turned and walked off. "Let me be first to apologize. I had no idea—"

"—Girl Please," Michelle cut in. "You know how I was," she laughed. "I was so overtop with all that bestie stuff. We were acting like boyfriend and girlfriend," she said dismissing the matter with a wave of the hand.

Rachel kept quiet for a minute. She still had Michelle's brain to pick, but momentarily lost interest in why she was there. Her conscience was busy getting bigger, trying to figure out what went wrong between them, when she should have been leaving the past in the past, to figure out a spin for her debut book. But it wasn't easy reconciling Michelle's behavior. How could a person she thought she really knew, be so off the page, and that far behind in the same book they had once read together?

Feelings aside, lunch went well. The food was delicious. The ambiance warm. And the service, as usual, flawless. Michelle brushed over the details of the man she married, describing Vin as a handful, always up in the air about one thing or the other. Despite their ups and downs she claimed she still loved him. Together they made the cutest boys she wouldn't trade for the world. "Guurrl, I think that man might kill me if I tried to leave him with his sons!"

The remark was unsettling to think the less, until she remembered HOPE, and Nina. Not everyone was in need of saving, especially women who thought nothing of doting over an abuser, playfully describing this social sore as a handful. But then too, angry as she was to see Michelle's ignorance had tripled, (save for the napkin she caught her using), in under an hour her own conscience had quadrupled. Over calamari, scallops, crab-cakes and a coherent vantage point she was giving Michelle's perspective renewed consideration.

She had to face it. The job was turning into something she hadn't anticipated. She sucked at this type reporting. Be damned if dirty scoops were what readers craved. Drug addicts also craved narcotics, which interestingly enough, drug dealers and media magnets did have one thing in common. No conscience. She did, and it had grown. No longer did she care about writing the book Wendy thought interesting. In fact, she started contemplating burying both Michelle and Wendy in her past.

She wanted to tell stories to increase awareness, and lift spirits, and hopefully entertain in the process, supposedly Voices' mission. Where, or how, someone along the way dropped that ball she didn't know, but got so caught up in the fantasy she started speaking out loud. "Well, while you've been happily playing house, I'm about to write that book I always wanted to write," she announced. Finally going to get my name out there."

"Alright Rocky, good for you," Michelle chirped, pouring her 3rd Elvis over her sorbet. "Guurl, the food was good but these drinks don't taste like nothing but water," she explained. scooping up the last of her sorbet she had poured her 3rd Elvis over.

"Shelly, are you sure you're going to be able to drive," she asked concerned.

"I ain't driving," Michelle shot back, the least bit fazed by the alcohol she had sucked down since sitting down. And this didn't include all the 'water' she drank while waiting on her. "Vin dropped me off. I'm about to text him now," she said.

Rachel could not get over this new Michelle. Someone had swapped out her ex for this urbanized, distracted air head. It was no act. She truly was clueless.

"...So, what's your book about," she continued, seeming as unfazed with Rachel's revelation as she was with the shots she'd been throwing back.

"Well, that's why I called you," Rachel replied. "I kind of want to write about us, and how I almost dropped out of school trying to save you," and she paused... "...from possible sex—"

"—Whaaadt," Michelle giggled, though staring in her hand as she tapped on her phone.

Rachel couldn't tell if she was speaking to her or the phone, until she started repeating back some of what she heard.

"Wait. What? Who was you trying to save from sex!?!"

"You," Rachel replied. "I was trying to save you —"

"—Me," she burst out laughing. "Save me from SEX!?!"

"Sex-trafficking," Rachel corrected. "You didn't let me finish. I was pretty messed up thinking you were in trouble."

"Oh my gosh," Michelle gasped, shirking her eyes as she

went back to tapping the phone. She acted surprised but was more invested in what was happening in her lap. "Well, I'm sure glad you got out of that phase," she said, voice traveling from miles away.

Rachel was glad she wasn't listening. None of it mattered anyway. It was all water under a bridge, or a dam that already burst. One day this was going to be a bad chapter in a forgotten book. Graciously she admired the waiter's haircut and asked for the check after declining a doggy bag for her half-eaten cobbler.

Meanwhile, Michelle's face stayed planted in her phone. She was so focused on her virtual company she didn't notice her man headed towards them, but Rachel did. She remembered the beige face, the thick arrow brows and the old knife cuts across his face. He wasn't a tall man but diners looked up as he strolled by wearing a black leather mid-length jacket, the kind that looked like he spent a hundred bucks on but only wore once a year, and on Easter. Looked like he was about to whip out a gun, which she breathed a sigh of relief when he only whipped off the shades when he got to their table.

"Who you texting," he said, playfully grabbing Michelle by the shoulders as he leaned over to kiss her forehead... and read her phone.

Immediately she looked up squealing, "I've been trying to text you. I just texted Pac to see where you were..."

"I told you I was on my way," he replied.

"Unt un..." she argued. "No you didn't—"

"—Check your voicemail."

The two went back and forth playfully bickering like this for longer than charming, obviously showing off. But Rachel was hardly impressed, though grateful he didn't seem to remember their last encounter.

"Vin, this my girl Rocky," Michelle said after ignoring her for three-quarters of the lunch. "We go way back," she added.

Vincent greeted her in familiar city slang that those who knew the streets used, "hey...hi you doin'. Wassup?"

Cursorily she looked over, smiled and raised a hand without moving her arm. She was glad the bill had come during their foreplay. Examining the check kept her legitimately preoccupied. She had pulled out her cheat-tip card when Michelle spoke up.

"I told you I'm going to get that," Michelle said, though made no attempts to reach across the table to get anything.

"Too late," Rachel wryly teased, slipping her credit card into the bill-fold and passing it to the waiter. Dinner was a little over $100, not bad. Except, adding Michelle's drink tab, along with a healthy 25% tip for a gracious waiter nervously doing the dance all

17...

Whatever Rachel thought, Michelle thought differently. First off, like it was presented from the start, and she expressed over lunch, there would have been no issue had Rachel and all her lifesaving concerns had wanted to go to school together. She lost her then, when she was talking the long-distance friendship stuff. And if she really was listening and heard her, she would have known she didn't care for school in the first place. So Rachel could miss her with that bleeding crying heart smack talk.

But her and Vin left the seafood grill riding clouds...and this high not all alcohol related either. She was excited because Vincent was happy, an almost odyssey for him. Twenty-four/7 he stayed on soap boxes fussing about everything under the sun. But now he had an outlet to vent and be heard. She couldn't wait to rush this news over to Mermaid Lane and throw it all around that chilly house she grew up in. The following day it's exactly what she did. Dressing her little guys in matching cashmere sweaters, and 24-karat gold rope necklaces they'd gotten as Christmas gifts from their daddy, she took them to see their grandmother.

"Ma, Vin is about to have a book written about him," she walked in the house bragging.

Julia though, barely looked at her. Teton, the oldest, was getting so tall. Every time she saw him, it looked like he'd grown an inch. And was a handsome young man too. Big blue eyes. Beautiful golden curly locks. And she didn't know of a sweeter more pleasant well-mannered child. He was all 'yes ma'am, no ma'am'. She didn't know where he picked up the manners ...being raised by bums who thought it appropriate to weigh babies down with thick chains wrapped around their necks.

"He already makin' some tapes, because he not good with that whole paper and pen thing," Michelle carried on, well into picturing the outcome of her life partner finally getting the recognition and respect he so long deserved. Everyone who ever dismissed him, discounted him or painted him into dark corners was now going to have to recognize a king, and that included her mother.

But Julia had long since dismissed her daughter's odd bantering. She was wrapped up in her grandsons, at the moment bouncing baby Marcellus on her knee while trying to help Ryker out of his coat. The child's zipper was stuck and he was getting impatient trying to free himself to get at the boxes beneath her Christmas tree. Not all of the gifts were for him, but he didn't know this, nor cared.

"Wait...hold still," she told Ryker, amused at him yanking the zipper left and right. "Let grammy help you," she chuckled, ignoring Michelle's old rusty windchime sound.

"Rocky's going to write it for him, and get some people she know to publish it," Michelle broadcasted, singing and slurring her words, playing up the urban hip-hop chick, sashaying around her mother's dining room table popping her lips and plucking kalamata olives off a tray and in her mouth. The hor'dourves spread was for friends Julia had invited over later that afternoon, what irked her to the hair follicles watching her child with those extra wide hips picking over the food with her filthy nasty fingernails.

Regardless of what the family claimed, Michelle wasn't raised like this. She attended the best schools, was read to every night, and up until she left for Brown, she looked and spoke like a decent young lady taught proper etiquette.

"Ma, you hear me," Michelle giddily squealed. "Rocky's going to get Vin a book deal!" She couldn't see her mother's face, not that she really needed to, but if she had eyes behind her back, she would have seen Julia snarl and roll her eyes before replying, "oh, that's nice honey!"

"You know Rocky always wanted to write...I'm so happy for her...she works over there on the Main Line at the TV station," she gushed on, not caring an iota about whether her facts were straight or not. This, however, would have been explosive news for Rachel who, for more reasons than one, may have died had she been a fly on the wall. At that very moment she was in her apartment thinking Michelle hadn't heard a word she said.

But Michelle wasn't done. She was just catching her first wind. She couldn't wait to stick it to her mother, and turn the blade for the way Julia treated Vincent. "Now he can get his story...the whole story... out there," she emphasized. "Er'body walkin' around here with they butts up in the air like they stuff don't stink, gonna feel his name," she added with particular triumph.

Yeah, Julia knew just who she was talking about…and she knew why too. Six years later and Michelle was still salty about the way she treated Vincent and his family during Teton's birth. They didn't want to come over to her house in the first place. It took a lot for Vincent to work up courage to meet a supremacy he couldn't smack in the mouth if the situation called for it.

He, along with Serge, Fe-Fe, and his mother Voge showed up to the house. They brought along bouquets of flowers; hand-picked yarrows, daisies and colorful plants Voge grew in their backyard. It wasn't the prettiest corsage, but was the thought that counted, making what Julia did unforgivable. It would have been one thing if they tried to beat her down with the stems. There, however, was no defense to taking those flowers and throwing them in the garbage. She didn't even wait for them to leave.

Naturally Michelle had a score to settle, the reason she showed up, unannounced, ten in the morning with the kids dressed in clothes Vincent preferred to see them dressed in. "He's putting all the people he like in his book…you know…like all the people he consider human," Michelle clarified, doing her best to double over her mother and knock the wind out of her.

Julia only rolled her eyes. Michelle was hardly hurting her feelings. She had her own version of Teton's birth. For starters, there wouldn't have been a need for Vincent, or his family to visit, had not Michelle needed a clean place, free of rodents and unhinged barbarians to recuperate from childbirth. And damn right she dumped those weeds in the trash! That's where weeds belong. She thought she was doing them a favor. But don't think she had forgotten what happened shortly after Ryker's birth.

Her and Michelle were barely speaking when Ryker was born. About a month later, Teton barely walking, Michelle showed up on her doorstep…hair all over her head, face swollen, and smelling like she hadn't bathed in months. She didn't hesitate to grab her grandbabies. They didn't deserve what Michelle was putting them through. By the grace of God they were okay, because she wasn't sure what to make of the situation seeing their bloody blankets and trickle of blood leading up the driveway. Disheveled as Michelle looked, those two sweet innocent little faces were the only reason she opened the door that morning. And a couple of days later, when that gangster-strutting thug showed up at her home, it took every ounce of civility she had in her not to pull the trigger.

At one point, while Michelle was going on and on about the book, Julia suggested she tell Rachel to check with her if she needed an impartial view to the story she was writing. The insult flew over her child's head.

"No ma, this Vin's story...and he will be tellin' it like it is," she clamored, explaining how he was going to include names, along with how he was going to restore his father's honor...and what he was wearing to interviews.

Julia looked at her child, sadly. Each time she saw her, she liked her a little less. If it weren't for her grandsons, the only real reason she had left to breathe, she wouldn't even be talking to this person. "Greaaat," she sang anyway, through a razor thin smile. She would say anything to continue seeing her grandbabies. "So, what else is Rachel up to nowadays?"

"Far as I could tell, nothing but some dead-end job," Michelle replied, shrugging as she popped another olive in her mouth. "She looked a little sad if you ask me. That's why I'm glad I didn't go the college route," she happily lopped on. "...All them years wasted and life just passing right by her..."

If Julia hadn't been holding her grandbaby in her lap she just might've vomited. "...And so, I guess you still trust her with your husband's life story?"

"What do you mean," Michelle asked, her face contorted. "It ain't like I'm trustin' her to hold a bag of cash or somethin'..." she huffed, rolling her eyes as she popped another olive in her mouth. "It ain't even all that serious!"

18...

If Rachel really were a fly, and had been on that wall, the exchange between her and Wendy may have ended differently. But she had been nowhere in the room with Michelle and her mother when she got, what could be considered, the last rites from Wendy. It started in email, Rachel giving Wendy the standard two-week's quit-notice in two short sentences. Her phone rang almost immediately.

"Are you okay," Wendy asked. She sounded concerned, but not desperate.

"I don't know," Rachel replied, before describing her lunch with Michelle …and the guy referred to as a handful. She tried her best to be 'that reporter' an executive deemed worthy to read, but feared she failed miserably. "I would've said anything to get out of there," she sighed.

Wendy chuckled. "Well then, I guess we won't be sending you to Syria or any place close to it anytime soon."

Rachel blinked, and swallowed. She had just sent over her resignation. But it didn't sound like Wendy had received it. She wondered if she should mention it, or wait and see where the conversation was going...since the email indeed was in her sent folder.

"Let's meet tomorrow, in my office…7AM," Wendy said. "I don't accept resignations by email."

Click!

Rachel paced around her 973-square foot apartment almost 8 hours, a full days' work, beating herself up over the call. The four years she interned with Brand Voices she had only heard of the infamous Wendy…and Gina, but never saw them, except for of course, their images gracing magazine covers, the Internet, and significant portions of wall space about as big as her apartment. When she came on board full-time, the illusive sightings pretty much continued... until Liz and Michelle upped their visibility.

Her imagination wasn't developed enough to guess what the meeting was going to entail. She hadn't experienced enough of Wendy to take so much as a wild guess. All she had was logic to go on. And common sense told her that a woman who's calendar was booked in years, would not waste her time on an entry-level employee where there was no gold-mine nearby.

This time she entered the office and noticed the spotless white walls, and the mahogany credenza on which neat stacks of paper covered the surface. The chairs surrounding Wendy's massive desk looked a little cheap, like furniture suited for a patio, but they were comfortable.

"You said a lot the other day, that got me to thinking," Wendy began, without the typical 'hello...how are you...please have a seat' greeting. She just dove right into it, as perhaps, any executive as busy might do.

"I really liked your angle...where you were taking your little story with your friend and that guy," she continued, luring Rachel to lean in. She didn't care for the 'little story' bit, but was all ears on hearing Wendy liked something she wrote.

"I just don't think you know what you have stumbled on. But if you're not interested in really going deep into the Brasco assignment," she carried on, using four fingers for quotes, "you may want to spend a little time out west writing about what you discover searching for what happened to your sister."

Every hair on Rachel's body stood. If she had a mirror in front of her, all she would see was eyes. The temperature in the room must have shot up a hundred degrees because she started sweating instantly. While mentioning Kelly's name became a banned topic within her family, Kelly stayed on her mind. Initially she thought her disappearance had something to do with her mother embarrassing the family, and the community, her colleagues and pretty much everyone for that matter. But over time she didn't get why Kelly would cut everyone out of her life, especially her sisters. She used to watch a lot of investigative crime programs, as a sort of homage to her sister, always wanting to know what happened to her, but to hear Wendy so callously mentioning her, took her trauma to another level.

And yet, what really grabbed her by the shoulders and gave her a good shake was Wendy giving this project a name. There obviously had been a lot of discussion going on behind her back. She took her time to think...with both eyes closed...trying to find her center. She learned this breathing practice from counselors when she was going through the 'Michelle withdrawal.' She found it, but then lost it when she opened her eyes to see Wendy blithely doing work on her computer. The woman didn't give one coot about her feelings, and probably wasn't concerned whether she wrote any book at all. After a minute or so she spun around and asked, "so, what's it going to be?"

Too choked up to reply, she stammered trying to find her center again. She needed the job. She liked the money and the freedoms it afforded her. She had a cozy place of her own, a reliable car, and was building a little nest egg that could afford spending 250 on lunch with a friend she wasn't sure she even liked. The deal-breaker however was, like who, more so than her, wanted to write a book?

Wendy read all of this, with her face in the computer and fingers gaily dancing across the keyboard. Her level of awareness was reflected in her next comment. "Look Rachel," she said, looking over at her without an ounce of sympathy, "...life is full of choices. Nobody is going to give you a couple hundred thousand dollars to decorate your home and snack on lobster without making you work for the money. All these people you hear crying about the white man holding them back, look at 'em. Each and every one of 'em sit on their asses their entire lives letting others make choices for them!"

Not that she entirely agreed with her attitude, she sat there at that very moment juggling a handful of choices. No matter which one she chose, she saw a dark lonely road.

"I'll stick with Brasco," she quietly replied. Having talked with Michelle and meeting her handful that had already hijacked her story, this had to be the lesser of other evils.

"Good," Wendy said, wrapping up their 10-minute meeting. "You should see your advance in a couple of weeks. Meanwhile, before the end of the day I'll send you a work-summary so you know exactly what we want from that guy."

It was probably a million ways to get through a dark tunnel, one for every person who found themselves in one. Shriveling up in a corner...running back and forth...running in circles... doing cartwheels... screaming...raising both fists and punching the dark ...skipping along...dancing in place...as Wendy declared, the choices people made had range. She left the building walking, and then raced home to call her soft shoulder to cry on.

"I'm a nervous wreck," she confided to Kim. "I can't eat, sleep! Lord, I can't think! What on earth have I gotten myself into!?!

"Whoa," Kim interrupted, her voice raised like two open palms fending off blows. "Slow down sis. What happened?"

She explained, beginning with how she was about to quit, before hopping a high fence to ramble about her fallout with Liz, and the verbal beating she levied on an executive, that miraculously she wasn't fired for, but was actually promoted, which really wasn't a promotion. She actually was assigned to the worst section in the company, though she saw the move as an opportunity of a lifetime, since it was rare editors, especially entry-level, got to work from home for a whole month!

Kim didn't interrupt once. She let her vent for a full 5-minutes. And Rachel vomited all matters Wendy, Liz, Michelle and her handful, and publishing books, along with an assignment that came out of the blue. She described the full hour and a half lunch with Michelle in about 3 or 4 seconds. It was a record-setting ramble, though most miraculous, was she didn't need to take a breath, and was still breathing when Kim finally interrupted.

Everything made perfect sense to her. "Girl, maybe you should switch careers and try to become an opera singer or something," Kim laughed.

"Sis, this is not funny," Rachel sighed. She wanted guidance, not jokes. "I think I might just go on and quit anyway."

"Why!?!" Kim shrieked.

"Because! They're in there playing games," Rachel fussed. "It's a sick business. I thought Voices was about uplifting women! Making the world a better place! It's their mission statement for Christ's sake…what they supposedly cut their teeth on, but instead they are—"

"—Hang on," Kim cut in, raising her voice some. "You've got to lose some of the emotion," she said. "You're no longer a kid. Nobody is getting paid to hold your hand and walk you through every single decision."

And all be damn if Wendy hadn't said the same thing. Not that she saw her and Wendy becoming the ideal sculpture of sisterhood one day. That woman had already shown her she could cut her as well as hug her. But hearing the same wisdom in close symmetry gave her a new respect for Wendy.

"Remember what you told me…" she heard Kim asking. Of course she couldn't remember. It was a 20-something year relationship they shared; accounting for a lot of words exchanged between them.

"You told me you're not spending decades at the bottom," Kim reminded her.

Rachel remembered, and wanted to walk every single word backwards. "But I was just a kid," she whined. "I didn't know—"

"—Ugh, congratulations toots," Kim teased. "You've just been promoted," she laughed. "Look," she sighed, about to rub on the balm. "I know you don't agree with a lot of what happened to mom, but mom was right about one thing," and she paused for effect. "This is God speaking. This is your moment."

"I doubt it," Rachel disagreed. "If that's true, then me and a bunch of people want to know why innocent people are hurt."

"You're kidding me, right," Kim sighed.

No, she wasn't kidding, even if she skipped over a major part of her anxiety. Each time her mouth formed the perfect sphere, ready to let the words flip...fall...tumble out, her jaws clamped down and her lips collapsed. She kept trying but just couldn't get Kelly's name over her tongue. And it wasn't that Kim might not be able to handle what Wendy had mentioned. Knowing her sister and all who she knew, Wendy's revelations likely wouldn't be a revelation at all. It was she who wasn't ready to disturb her field of view, not when she thought she saw an itty-bitty light at the end of the tunnel.

"I just wished people would stay still...and stop with all this secrecy and back-stabbing, cutthroat stuff," she whimpered.

"In your business," Kim spat.

"In every business," Rachel shot back.

"Yeah, okay..." Kim chuckled. "Good luck with that. Maybe you'll be the one to find the cure for cancer too."

She backed out of her parking space, facing a relatively pleasant building she sighed deep breaths of relief every time she parked in front of, full of anxiety about meeting Vincent Cabrera. Her fingers crossed, hoping like never before, she'd give up her desire to return to her apartment with the same feeling.

According to the work-summary Wendy emailed, this guy was one of the greatest menaces to society. He'd been arrested over 149 times. She couldn't think of a crime he hadn't been accused of committing. All the major crimes were covered in the summary. He owed the state an astronomical figure. The number unpronounceable. He would die in debt, images she struggled to shake. How a person was allowed to freely walk around with his record illuded her, and wrecked her nerves to think she was about to sit down and talk with such a character.

They agreed to meet at the main public library. There were plenty of private rooms, and plenty of guards too, in case he decided to round out his arrest record. How Michelle managed to live with a guy like this was beyond her, so she wasn't taking any chances. She used three days leading up to the interview to prepare. She didn't spare a second agonizing over every single detail. Like what she would wear. A turtleneck and sneakers. And how she would handle the questions he didn't want to answer. Move on…use her creative writing skills to fill any holes. If she smelled alcohol, or sensed he was drunk or high, she was faking an asthma attack and mailing or emailing the questions, whichever he preferred. She had rehearsed every possible scenario, except one, or maybe hundreds of one.

She hadn't counted on getting into a big argument with her conscience. The debate started when she passed a police precinct and was reminded of stories from HOPE residents. One glance took her from 10, a barrel of anxiety blaming everyone she knew for why Vincents were on the street, to 110, convinced if she, alone, didn't do something, the world was going to hell. Essentially she was back in the tunnel, choosing a way to get through the anxiety, because if anyone was to be blamed for anything, it was her. She was the one who accepted the assignment, so eager to write a book that compromising a few values, and maybe even her sanity and life, was worth the sacrifice.

By the time she arrived at the main library and found 2-hour parking she was so far outside insanity that nobody could have told her she wasn't judge, jury and master of Vincent's fate. She hopped out of her car and walked at a sprinters pace down the street and around a corner to find the roughneck standing at the top of the steps waving and grinning. She didn't wave back, but if he could read the misty fog bubbles escaping her mouth with each breath she took climbing the steps he would have heard, 'buddy, I'm taking your crown!'

But then, as she almost reached the landing she made the mistake of looking up again. Seeing the translucent eyes of a tiger she tripped, and fell into his tunnel. From that point on there was no doubt she was going to be doing a whole lot of juxtaposing.

"Did you get lost trying to get here," he chuckled.

That was one positive about him and his Che-Che. They were not on colored people's time. "Yeah, it doesn't seem like the city put a lot of thought into people being able to visit this place," she replied, the anger gone but annoyance taking its time to fall off.

For some reason he looked a lot shorter than she remembered. And slimmer too. But not any less menacing. He still wore the leather jacket, except this time she noticed a cross tattooed on, or near his left temple. Geez, the visual was unnerving.

"Yeah, you suburban girls ain't familiar with 'dis part of 'da city," he laughed, opening a large brass door and holding it open to allow her to enter first.

"Thank you," she politely said, with an urge to step on his foot, hard. Maybe he might have a quip for how clumsy suburban girls were too.

There was a metal detector, and guards at the entrance, which he seemed rehearsed in the drill. He threw his wallet in the bin and proceeded to walk through the metal detector, hands up as if he'd just been read his rights. It beeped and the guard motioned him back.

"Oh Chief, it's just my phone," he replied, reaching deep into his pocket and pulling out a phone to hold up.

The guards looked at each other, and then him, but said

nothing. She panicked. The guy needed to be searched. He needed to be spun around, laid flat on the ground, spread eagle and with a foot in his back, every one of his pockets turned inside out and rigorously searched. Heck, hold that joker up by his ankles and shake him like an ugly ragdoll.

But none of that happened. The guard waved him through, and with a roll of the eyes and irritated sigh waved her through too. She got the distinct feeling, even though no bells sounded on her, the guards thought they were together, as in together-together. If she didn't really believe before, she knew then, why Wendy was so eager about this book assignment. She was about to work with a real tycoon and tyrant in one.

In a small room she asked if it was okay to record their conversation. "Naw," he replied. "I already made some tapes." Promptly he dug in both pockets and tossed a handful of 3x3 tape cartridges, from each pocket, across the table.

She squinted, trying to figure out what exactly she was looking at. She wasn't that old, but hadn't seen these cassettes since she used to pull them out of her parent's answering machine when she didn't want them to know one of her teachers had called. A dozen of them used to come in a pack. She remembered that too. Because she kept a bunch of them scattered in her closet, buried beneath piles of paper her parents never bothered to search.

"You ain't never seen 'dem kind of tapes, huh?"

The real question was, what did he expect her to do with them? She picked one up from the small pile and turned it over, marveling how tiny it was. Two fingers and a thumb completely concealed it. "Umm...I'm sure I can—"

"—It goes in one of 'dem... 'dem," and he snapped his fingers trying to recall the name of the contraption it fit. That's when she slipped back into his tunnel, and got a close look at his razor sharp eyes, and inch long lashes. He was a handsome 'dawg'... in his day. He probably had ladies lined up and wrapped around a block hoping to be his Valentine. But fast forward to this meeting, he didn't look like much. Up close his hair didn't look as greasy, but his nails sure did, and though she knew he had teeth, by the shape of his mouth, she couldn't be sure. Far as she could tell, it looked like tar in his mouth. She didn't know how Michelle kissed the guy, much less made three babies with him. She wouldn't let him touch her with a 10-foot pole.

"Oh, it's cool," she replied, quickly hopping out of his tunnel before he caught her staring. "We have all kinds of machines in the office. I'm sure we can—"

"—Wait now, hol' up," he interrupted, reaching across the

table and touching her arm. She didn't jump, but instantly looked down at his hand…the one with the scabby ashy knuckles. So much for what she wouldn't do. Somebody call 911. She just sat there and stared!

"Look! I don't want nobody listening to 'deez tapes until I see 'dat book," he argued, removing his hand to bang on the table, karate chopping fashion. He didn't hurt the table, or his hand. He used just enough force to get her attention.

"Yeah, but—" She was about to promise no one would hear the tapes, but he cut her off.

"—Naa, Naa… ain't gonna be no buts," he spat, a pebble of spit narrowly missing her, landing on the table just north of her hand she immediately jerked back. He didn't seem to notice because he kept talking.

"I know Che-Che cool wid' you, but 'deez words got to stay between me and you 'til I see somefin' on paper."

This guy was serious. She paid attention to how rigid his fingers were, double-jointed and curled backwards. He was wearing a wedding band too. It was a simple gold ring, unlike the rope around his wrist. That chain must've set him back, or cost somebody, a fortune… the figure he owed the state suddenly magnified in her head.

As he lamented on how he wanted the project to go, a pen rolled off the table. She leaned over and picked it up, noticing he was wearing white tube socks…and black dress shoes. She didn't know the brand or maker, but the lace ups were clean and appeared to be the type shoes that needed a nightly polish to hold a shine.

He was still talking when she raised up with the pen. Not that she had been gone for long, but he didn't seem to notice she had been gone at all. In a psychology class she had taken at Penn, she learned people exhibiting his type behavior likely suffered from a traumatic episode. She recalled their prior (actually traumatic introduction) and remembered him talking about seeing his father killed. At that moment her heart sank. Bravely she reached across the table and touched his hand. Instantly he stopped talking and looked down. His grin turned her stomach, but after coolly pulling her hand back she promised him no one was going to hear those tapes. "I only need to get a tape recorder so that I can hear them," she said.

He was still grinning, though sizing her up, reading her from the inside. "I bet you think I can't read, don't you?"

She never thought about it, but since he asked, she would assume that, however, nothing she would say to his face. So, she shrugged.

"You ever read 'Autobiography of an Ex-Colored Man?'

She hadn't, and admitted as much.

"I liked 'dat book," he exclaimed. "You kind of remind me of 'dat story...like you don't know whether you want to be white or black."

He got a rise out of her on that remark. "I don't want to be anything," she snapped. "It's everybody else who want to choose who I am."

"Don't get mad at me," he clapped back. "Why you tryna' kill 'da messenger. I didn't do it," he laughed. "But you lucky. At least you can pick which one you want to be."

"Oh, so that's what the book was about?"

"Sort of," he replied, shrugging as if he could care less, about either the book or the question. "The dude just wanted to know how people get treated different based on 'dey skin color. You ever have 'dat happen to you?"

She tried to answer but couldn't quite give him the answer he wanted because she didn't relate people's skin color to why she was treated a certain way. She only defined them as jerks, friends, or back-stabbers. And oh, one more. People who minded their business. But she refrained from spelling this out because she started picking up on this hot and cold, and on and off side to him. One minute he talked like someone might describe the weather, and the next second he was talking like she had touched a nerve. Obviously he surprised her, being able to elaborate on so many books. He was right about that. She would've never guessed. She hadn't heard of Bill Campbell, Iceberg Slim, Van Whitfield and a cherry-picking of others. But this didn't mean that Petry, Sister Souljah, Zane and a diverse list of females were less than. Once she almost came within a thread of cutting short the interview when he told her females didn't write as well as men!

"Maybe you might want to find a man to write your story," she suggested in the creamiest tone anger could create.

"I already tol' you, I don't want nobody hearin' 'deez tapes but you!"

And if he knew how to comprehend, he would've heard he could take his mini mountain of tapes and deposit them in a space where men didn't shine. Of course she wouldn't have dared expressed this, out loud or written across her face, and for more reasons than the thought of being accidentally spat on again.

"No one is going to read or hear anything until I finish the first draft," she coolly replied. Her voice never cracked or dipped once. "But you have to let me know how you want the first draft."

She assumed on paper...and hopefully not chiseled on a rock or sent by morse code.

"Well, you can...you know...like...like..." and he got to snapping his finger again trying to recall a word...

"Transcribe," she gently inserted, a word he should have mastered, given his familiarity with books...and courts.

"Yeah, type up my voice...and I mean type up everything 'dat's on 'deez tapes... I don't want no'fin' left out. 'Den you can bring the book over to my house and leave it with Che-Che so I can look at it later on when I get home."

"Okey-doke," she replied rising from the chair, about to reach for the tapes.

"—Wait! Where you goin'?!" ...And he grabbed her hand, though it was the tape he really was going for. Her hand just became a casualty of war. "You jus' gon' leave like 'dat? 'Dats how you do business!?!"

First off, he needed to back up if he thought she, alone, could turn what looked like a nonstop day of listening to tapes into a hardback book. That wasn't how publishing was done.

Second order of business, he needed to get back in his lane. Probably from the day he bounced into the world, he ran "'da show". Everybody in his house listened to what he said, and did what he told them to do. But that was his house. This was her show. So don't try to lecture her about proper business etiquette, which she edited down to asking if he had any other questions... or had checked his pockets for more tapes.

He laughed, showing a mouthful of unidentified objects adhered to his gums. She couldn't tell if they were teeth, tattoos, bracelets or what. "Jus' let me know when I can expect to hear somefin' back?"

The guy acted like he was buying a car, but she replied, "I'll get back to you in about—"

"—Get back to me," he mocked.

"I mean, I'll email you if I have questions, but the assignment should be done in a month," she replied like she would to any boss where she didn't want to lose her job, or life over for disrespecting.

"A-ight, a-ight..." he said leaning back, opening his jacket and grinning wide. "I trust you..." he laughed. "I know where you work...and live," he smiled.

She might've flinched, or blinked, but she didn't react. He was toying with her. Playing her like a puppet. Like who was he kidding? She had his life in her purse.

Vincent and Michelle didn't talk much, which didn't necessarily construe a troubled relationship. It was just the way it was between them; Vincent parading her around when he wanted to show off his priciest arm charm, and simultaneously spoiling and terrorizing her to keep her genuinely happy at home. Their age and cultural gap didn't naturally allow for much conversation.

But when he returned home, he wanted to talk. "Che-Che, where you at ma'me!?!" he called out.

She was upstairs on the phone talking to Amora who was in her first year at NYU. Wasn't anything major going on. Amora just considered her, her greatest advocate...and confidant. She called a lot, and sometimes they talked for hours.

"I'm on the phone with Mora! I'll be down there in a sec," Michelle yelled back.

He grumbled. Wasn't no telling how long those two would be yakking on the phone. He plodded upstairs where he found her laid back on the bed, legs up crossed over the other at the knees. Eyes closed she was laughing at something Amora was telling her.

"Hey," he said, causing her to open her eyes and lift her head. "Tell her you'll call her back. I need to talk to you..."

Except for his family next door, almost everyone else who encountered them did not like the way he bossed her, acting more like a father who had this one much too late, instead of a loving spouse who considered her his equal, and them a husband-and-wife team. But this became their communication style. He talked and she listened, and obeyed. Much of the time he was out of the house, either working...or next door sleeping off a high. Their situation didn't begin like this, though. It took one night after throwing back a significant amount of Crown Royal, to rinse down some pills, and scaring the life out of her before their glue gelled.

He got home that particular night, arguing about why the front door was locked. It was two in the morning, that's why. But Michelle kept quiet, he was so off the floor. And she didn't dare go for the phone to call 911, because every cop in the nation had to have heard him. Amora, who still lived with them, ran in their bedroom pleading with her daddy, begging him to stop. The next day he apologized and vowed to stay next door when he'd been drinking. He loved his Che-Che to pieces and never wanted to see her that upset. In fact, he scaled back on drinking after that episode, making his working long hours the primary reason their exchanges were so few. That, and the fact she was no match for philosophical debates he liked to entertain. Indeed, he talked a lot, why she got off the phone right away. It was rare he demanded to talk.

"Did you ever find out where your friend lives?"

Michelle looked confused, and concerned, and with good reason. What friend? She didn't have any friends he didn't know where they lived. He was very observant about who she hung around. There was a girl he really hated. Her name was Sheila and she had a little boy about the same age as Teton and Ryker. They lived a few doors down, which gave her an excuse to be near his brother Paco who all the ladies fell over. The guy was young, dark chocolate and fine as hell. Every woman that locked eyes on him hung around his ankles, and Sheila was one. But despite what she really was after, Michelle liked the girl's company. Unlike the other trollops tramping in and out of Voge's house, she dressed nice and liked to talk about (and do) things that involved the boys. But Sheila was married, and Vincent didn't like no married woman hanging around his girl and pushing up on another man, be it his brother or another nigga. "I betta' not find 'dat bitch in here," he said one day, as if it was her sneaking around. "If I catch 'dat ho in here, 'ders gonna be a problem!"

That was the last of her dealings with Sheila, but not the last time he made it clear he had an eye on anyone he thought might threaten what they had together.

"Which friend," she asked, braced for a vigorous defense. She didn't want anyone threatening what they had either, even if there wasn't an army of people lined up at the door, eager to hang out, with his energy, or that well of family next door in the mix.

"'Dat girl who's writing my book," he replied.

"Oh," she sighed, relief instantly washing over her. "I don't know where Rocky stays. Probably over there on the Main Line where she works. Why? She stand you up?"

"Naa, I met up with her...with her stuck up self," he

scoffed. "I just want to know where she stay, in case she start acting funny."

"Well, let me call and find out," Michelle said. She opened her contacts and hit Rachel's number in one tap. But the call went to voicemail on account of Rachel being 15-20 minutes away from her apartment, smiling gratefully by what she deemed to be a great meeting. Things didn't go half as bad as she imagined when backing out of her parking space three hours ago. Her heart was still beating, a little faster than normal, but she was convinced whatever was on those tapes was going to make engaging literature, given she was already curious about his story.

And then she heard her phone humming, and after pulling into her parking space checked to see who's call she missed. Surprised it was Michelle, she called her right back. A fatal attraction type situation was the first thing that entered her mind. Michelle was probably checking up on her grinning husband with the ape-like knuckles, who hadn't made it home yet, thinking he was out two-timing her with her sour ex-bestie.

"Damn girl, you 'bout 'da hardest bitch to catch up with!" Nope. Wasn't that. At least her tone didn't strike her as being worried about her handful's whereabouts. But 'bitch'? She wasn't about to respond to that type greeting.

"How y'alls meeting go? Did you listen to his first tape? Girl, Vin deep. I keep telling him, he should run for office. He real knowledgeable about politics," Michelle rambled before hitting her with the real reason why she called. "So, where you live at?"

Rachel thought before answering. "I'm not home right now. Does he want the tapes back? I can meet him at my office," she said.

"Oh no, he...oh, I mean I was thinking about dropping by one day next week to catch up," Michelle replied. "I need to get out of this house and see something different," she added, satisfied with her quick fix.

Absolutely not. In a rhyme Dr. Suess might use, she did NOT want to see Michelle next week. She did not even want to see Michelle next month. She didn't care to see Michelle in any season. She didn't care to see Michelle for any reason. Forget the psychobabble psychologists talked and do-gooders fell for, she was not opening her home to another Nina. And if she wasn't on the hook for getting her handful's book to print, she would've hung up on her, or never answered her call to begin with.

"Oh, next week I'm going to be out of town," she quickly replied. "I usually don't get home until late anyway," she added for reinforcement. "Maybe—"

"—Maybe I can drop by tomorrow," Michelle piped in. "And don't worry about cleaning up," she laughed. "Remember. I live with three boys and no maid."

Perhaps Michelle used another kind of calendar because last Rachel checked, tomorrow was next week! What a complete air-head. But she might have been on to something, mentioning she had to get out. Staying home, jobless, raising three boys in a house the bank did not own, and upgraded every time she opened a home decor magazine and saw something she didn't have, sounded like realism was getting sucked right out of her already narrow mind. But Rachel wasn't hating. Must be nice to feel spoiled rotten by a man who for every mean word or crime he committed against her, giving her another diamond, or new floor, or appliance, or bulbous reason to believe fairytales existed.

And still, Rachel had nothing to say to a person like this, and definitely didn't want her, or her little boo-boos mistaking her insignificant living space she worked hard to afford and keep clean, for a place their daddy could fix up when he sobered up. "Fair warning," she sort of teased. "My place is small and not child-proof."

"Oh, don't worry about my boys," Michelle replied. "I'm taking them to my mom's tomorrow. She usually keeps them during the week, since they go to school over there."

And listen at that! Her mother basically was raising her boys! "All three," Rachel shrieked as if she really cared. "Must be nice," she added, seconds from claiming she had to take another call. The idea was to small-talk herself out of giving up her address. She knew who really wanted it.

"Yeah, but it would be nicer if she paid for the school too," Michelle sulked like the insatiable brat she had become. She never cared for education, and thus was no fan of Vincent spending $50K a year on her two oldest boy's education alone. The cost was going to climb, especially when the baby started school, money Michelle fussed she'd rather be spent elsewhere. She hardly wanted to roll around in an 11K eyesore that needed a club and didn't come with seat warmers.

Wow. Just wow! She couldn't help but blame Julia for creating this monster. All that time she thought she hated Mrs. Perkins for being too harsh and mean with Michelle. Turned out, she wasn't mean and harsh enough!

Bottom line, no one but someone like Vincent, who she so loved and adored, wanted to deal with a brat like this. "I'm so glad I met him," she said at one point. "If I hadn't met him, my little boo-boo wouldn't be here."

The comment, news to Rachel, struck her very odd. She

couldn't figure out which boo-boo was being referenced. "Oh, I thought you guys were married for a while," she probed.

"We have been. We got married in 09," she replied.

Hmmp. That really didn't jive, until Michelle volunteered the trouble she ran into at Brown. She was accused of stalking a rich white boy who was the one who raped, and got her pregnant. "Guurrl, him and his momma was tryin' to put me and my mom in cuffs," she casually confessed. "I just hope lil T— never asks about them people 'cause I'm sure gonna hate hurting his feelings."

It was a zipper moment. Rachel had no idea Michelle left school pregnant. She assumed all three boys belonged to her handful. Surprised by this revelation she asked Michelle if she knew who the father was.

"Yeah girl! I just told you," she argued. "...That punk I met at Brown! He lucky I didn't know Vin then!"

"Wow, that's so wrong," Rachel sighed, glad she hung on the line a minute longer. "It makes me sick when I hear—"

"—Girl, that's what I'm tryna' tell you. We got to get together and catch up. Where do you live?"

"Oh, I'm in Conshohocken," Rachel replied. "But I can meet you at—"

"—I know where that is," she blurted. "My pediatrician is in Broomall," she said like Rachel should have known this.

So, Rachel went on and gave her the address, just not the apartment number. "Make sure you call first," she warned. "I'm rarely home. I'm usually at my sister's house, or at work."

The call gave her a real incentive to listen to the tapes and write the book quickly as possible, and not that she needed the extra boost. She couldn't wait to roll out of bed, trading the heels for fluffy white cotton slippers, and enjoying a cup of good hot morning joe before sitting down in front of a keyboard. The office environment, and everything that went along with it, got old quick.

But first she needed to have something to play the tapes on. So, instead of going in the house, unwinding, and delving into the project first thing in the morning, she stuck the key back in the ignition, turned the car on, backed out of her parking space and drove straight to the one place where, at that hour, there was bound to be a free of charge device to play the tapes.

It was Sunday, about 8:30, almost 9PM when she got to work, so fewer people were in the building; none on the 2nd floor. Save for emergency lamps, it was dark and a little eerie getting to her desk.

She put her laptop on the docking station and powered it on before dashing to the kitchen to grab coffee. It was dark in there too, which meant turning on lights to hook up the coffee. Had she not wanted to risk bumping into anyone on the 3rd floor, asking a half dozen people "how are you," and one giving her a lengthy reply to a polite greeting, she could've skipped this step altogether.

But those weren't her choices. In the same manner she was about to decide on word choice, sentence structure and whether an introduction was necessary, was the same choice she made selecting her vices. And to the people who told her she was too young to be hooked on caffeine, were the very people who needed to get an exrta cup of coffee, find a seat, calm down and mind their business.

She was signing into the network, armed with a trusty hot cup of Verona Café, when Barry crept up behind her.

"What are you doing in here," chuckled a politely amused communications director.

"No, what are you doing DOWN here," she laughed back.

"I saw lights on and wondered what was going on."

Number one rule she learned working for Voices; refrain from discussing sensitive projects with anyone other than the project director...in this case Wendy. Depending on the nature of the project, until the job was complete, it sometimes was necessary to even censor what was told to the boss. There were a lot of reasons for this, which in this case Barry oversaw the publishing division of Brand Voices. If he was asking questions, then she needed to be careful about answering them.

"Where else would you go 9 at night on a Sunday for peace and quiet," she teased.

He laughed. It was the cry of every serious writer. Those who had no choice learned to work through noise, what made their cries even louder. But those who did have a choice...well... they might be found in odd places at odd times.

"I was just checking to make sure we didn't have a Watergate burglar," he teased too. "...Because if we did, I wanted to be first to get the scoop."

They both fell out laughing. "Look," Rachel said in the middle of their hardest laugh yet. "I was wondering if I could get access to the equipment room." This was what a good cup of coffee did. It helped her think of shortcuts. Like, why type up a request and have to wait on the authority to let her in the equipment room, when Barry was right there?

Without revealing exactly what she was working on, she showed him one of the tapes and asked if they might have a device that recognized it. He did. One of the storage rooms was filled with antique devices. He handed her a portable Walkman she could slip in her purse and take anywhere. "Thanks Barry," she giggled. "Now, can I borrow this? I'll probably need it for a few weeks..."

"Sure," he laughed. "If anyone is looking for that thing, it'll probably be a dinosaur!"

They cracked up laughing all over again. Barry was an older gentleman with the whole v-neck sweater vest, plaid pants and salt and pepper bozo hairstyle going on. Though he had the same nose as most other editors, his demeanor was that of a grandfather more interested in covering his grandchildren's graduations than stealing scoops for nefarious purposes... even if he did ask where she got the tapes.

"If I told you, I'd have to kill you," she joked, despite kind of being dead serious.

"Well, be careful," he warned. "Some stories are better left untold."

Leaving a partially deserted building at that hour with that type warning did not create the best energy, but she definitely thanked the gods for being able to pull up to a decent building with a coveted parking space. It was a negative and plus that allowed her to have mad respect for the Barry types, when truth to the matter, climbing corporate ladders with the grandfatherly advice was for old heads. She wanted to rise up the ranks like supersonic jets reached Mach ten.

And even so, she was a little spooked when she entered her apartment. It wasn't only Barry's advice, but the tail ending of her meeting with Vincent and his wife's subsequent phone call. Couple that energy with the new hire handbook she got from Voice, full of textbook lessons of what could happen to careless journalists, along with the experiences she learned at HOPE, had her turning on every light in the apartment.

After a quick shower, and another cup of joe, she got busy. She counted 18 tapes, none marked. All appeared to have seen better days. One was cracked, so she lined that one up last. It looked like ketchup stains on another, though it could have been dried blood. She put that one next to last. Most had partially, or completely missing memo stickers, where ordinarily a note that described what was on the tape would be noted. For instance, it would have been helpful had he numbered the tapes so she would know in what order to listen to them. But they weren't, so she created her own order, popping in and out tapes until she got to the obvious first tape; his introduction.

Vincent Julio Cabrera, 42, was born in Havana. He didn't remember much about his young life except... a lot of family, dirt streets, funky boat rides, murders, and the smell of his mother's sweat. He was the youngest of five boys; the first set of kids his mother had. During their travels he clung to her, tucked under her arm as she held onto her boys, singing the whole way during the roughest patches of their life.

Family was most important to him. In America was where he got his rudest awakening, when he saw his father murdered; at the hands of a man with a United States flag sewn on his uniform. He was 10, and hated police ever since. His father was only trying to tell the guards he didn't want to be separated from his family. The guards didn't care. They raised their weapons, dared his father to make a move, and when he did, bringing his hands up in prayer fashion, about to plead one more time, a guard pulled the trigger, shooting him dead in the center of his chest. He watched the greatest man he knew fall to his knees and slowly tumble over. While the family wailed, he looked down at his father, and into his eyes after one guard kicked him over with his boot. His father's eyes were open. With one tear falling from the corner of his eye, he looked just like Jesus.

Rachel choked up a little bit on that part. Right from the start she doubted how she was going to make it through the rest of the tapes, which looking over at the remaining tapes brought into view a caption Wendy said. "Do you know who that guy is..." She wasn't asking. It was a warning of what was to come.

His tone changed after his father's murder. It was the same voice, but a different narrator. He spoke of his mother Vogel, or Voge, and the curse she put on the guards for killing his father. He didn't believe in all that satanic stuff his mother and aunts talked, but witnessed many incidents that would make others a believer.

He was a kid when he first started getting threatened by this superstitious spirit that would 'get him' (alas 'the getti') if he misbehaved, or didn't do this or that. But he wasn't a believer. He'd seen and heard about a lot of death and destruction, the reason they left the island for the States in the first place. So, 'the getti' had a lot of people to get before him, if he was to fall for wrongs being righted that way.

And yet, as he looked back on his life, there wasn't a person who crossed his mother in a major way that didn't suffer from the 'getti' she put on them.

His favorite memory of how 'the getti' supposedly worked, was the time 'it got' a city worker. Earlier that day they had been in the welfare office dealing with a woman who had been particularly rude. Voge didn't speak English, and designated his oldest brother, Serge, to translate. The woman got nasty, telling Serge she wanted Voge to speak for herself, or schedule an appointment with another bureaucrat to do a proper translation. Of course, as in any emergency situation, particularly a few days before Christmas, the family didn't have time for all that. Except for food they scavenged from trash cans behind restaurants, they hadn't eaten in days. They were hungry, and desperate.

But the woman held her ground, smirking as they trudged out of the building and into a blizzard where Voge's eyes turned a bitter cold gray. They returned home, wet and cold, to a boarded up building they paid someone (out a window) $5 a day to stay in. Too frozen to be mad, sad or scared of anything, to include death, they huddled in a corner where the only thing working in that raggedy place were the windows. All two windows let in all the cold air that wanted to come in, leaving 3-inch sheets of ice on the walls.

The only one not huddled up was Voge. She sat in the center of the room on the floor, legs criss-crossed and rocking back and forth, talking to her 'getti'. A couple of hours later, to their surprise, the social worker showed up. Loaded with bags and bags of food and toys, and $300 in hard cold cash, plus a long apology, that woman had driven on four bald-tires, through six feet of snow to bring them Christmas. Vincent knew about the bald tires because it was him and his brothers who helped unload her Volkswagon. She blamed all the people who had gotten over on her before, for why she didn't believe Voge couldn't speak English. She never explained exactly what changed her mind though. She couldn't. But he and his brothers knew.

It wasn't the first, nor would be the last time when Voge's chanting turned a situation around... and without laying hands on anyone. Many lost livelihoods, minds and much more to 'the getti'. It was the main reason his father's people, though they made up other excuses, wanted nothing to do with her.

Goose bumps big as a goose itself crawled up and down Rachel's arms and back she was so chilled by how he described his mother, and 'the getti'. Even as he explained in a gravelly voice rasping up, likely due to what he was drinking while recalling, "yeah, I don't get off on all that voodoo stuff, but I don't fuck wid' it either," she could feel this woman's presence.

According to Vincent however, most people had nothing to worry about. He described his mother like a harmless watchdog, only provoked when warranted.

She started drifting, struggling to interpret his diction through the sipping he was likely doing, along with his habit of mixing city jargon with Spanish, French and Haitian Creole. He didn't talk fast, but said a lot. She had typed over 5000 words, with over a dozen more tapes to go. Exhausted, 'the getti' told her to turn out the lights and get some sleep...

She awoke to a panel of voices on TV arguing. That's one thing she always did. Slept with the TV on. Lights off, but TV always stayed on, unless of course, cable was out. Then she'd sleep with the lights on, or wouldn't sleep at all.

At any rate, it wasn't so much that she woke up to arguing, as it was this argument waking her up. A commentator sitting behind a desk was refereeing a knock down drag out fight between three "professionals", sitting in three separate boxes bickering, and loudly so, first thing in the morning, at around seven-ish, about rape culture. The woman, in the right box, with the long black hair looking much like a 'Rolling Stones' member, was going off about men taking advantage of women because they'd been getting away with it for so long. In her expert opinion, these men needed to be made examples of. Hung out to dry, to teach them right and wrong behavior to protect women and end rape culture once and for all. She was on a roll, pointing out how she'd been taught in law school, almost all convicted criminals had done what they were accused of before. "Larry," she scowled, "there's always a pattern, Larry! Little boys are watching!"

Rachel sat up, reminded of Michelle casually talking about her experience at Brown. It crushed her hearing about the incident, and crushed her more listening to Michelle talk, period. But who'd want to defend Michelle's of the world!?! Little girls looked up to them too. Women who, like Nina, should know better than to invite an ex who threatened to kill her, to the home of another woman who opened her home to protect her and her children.

The topic hit a sore spot because the argument defended women who weren't talking about being dragged from cars in broad daylight, or assaulted in the middle of the night by strangers who entered their homes through closed, locked doors, or children living in abusive situations that didn't get air until the child escaped their captor, or felt safe to talk, or put in rehab, or jail, or got pregnant, or worse. These were very different victims from those giving away their power, be it voluntarily or naively. The screaming she woke up to reminded her of situations she experienced at HOPE. And not that any woman feeling victimized didn't deserve an ally, if for nothing more than, "NO, ALWAYS MEANT NO, PERIOD!"

In many respects, she was on board with the screaming woman, who she wiped her eyes to read on screen was a scholar from Duke. Usually scholars, particularly from upstate, weren't so animated, but this one was. Her brows resembled boomerangs and her nostrils could blow out a full grown rhino; one woman that for sure hadn't lost a sliver of power, one reason Rachel was on her team. And then the guy in the left box chuckled, "of course, there's always a pattern. Who, by the time they've reached adulthood, hasn't had sex!?!"

"But that's not what we're talking about here, Clive, and you know it," fumed the Duke Professor.

"Oh, but it's exactly what you're saying," refuted Clive. "You're saying every guy who is accused of a sex crime has a sexual past, which more often than not, IS TRUE!"

Rachel barely heard Clive's point because of the shouting. Everyone was rocking and rolling, talking over the other. And yet, Rachel didn't miss the overall beat.

She wanted to find that guy who impregnated Michelle. The Duke Professor might've known him. He came from her community. Surely his family would like to meet one of their youngest heirs. Might be a pattern?

Rachel was within a heartbeat of pressing send on the email she quickly drafted to Wendy when, for some odd reason the tapes on the table caught her attention. At a glance it looked like one cassette was missing. She knew this because she had lined them up even-steven. Now they were lined up, uneven-steven. She sighed a breath of relief when it dawned on her the missing cassette was probably still in the recorder. Just to be sure, before hitting send, she hopped up and popped open the door on the recorder. Her heart back flipped and, like opening her purse in a grocery store, about to pay the cashier, and no wallet, she panicked.

She recounted the tapes. And looked beneath the table ... and around the table, and then around the kitchen...laying on the floor to look beneath the stove and refrigerator, going as far as to closely examine the checkered floor pattern. She retraced her steps around her itty-bitty living space, 973-square-feet of space in total, not much room to get lost in, even if the tapes had feet. Maybe she miscounted the tapes to start with? So, she recounted them, for the fourth time. Rechecked beneath the table...around the kitchen... her robe pockets...the bed...drawers...she checked everywhere!

Things like this annoyed her. She wasn't a hoarder. And was incredibly organized, to the point of OCD. She literally had four pieces of furniture, five if the TV mounted on the wall were counted. A bed. A couch. One dresser, and a kitchen table. She also had two wastebaskets; one in the bathroom, and one beneath the kitchen sink. There weren't many reasonable places to check.

Right away everyone and everything became suspect. Barry could have gotten nosey, or maybe by accident had slipped the tape she showed him in his pocket, while pulling the tape recorder off the shelf. And there was Vincent, who could've been up to something. It was probably why he didn't check his pockets as she instructed him to do. Of course she rejected both scenarios, since she distinctly recalled counting the tapes, and lining them up on her kitchen table... AFTER... getting home.

That left Voge. And, oh boy, did not every hair stand at attention on that thought.

Determined ghosts, magic, sock puppets and 'gettis' were not real, Michelle being prima facie proof, given not one of those pokes (thank goodness) seemed to affect her, she decided the missing tape never existed. She simply miscounted, or had misaligned the cassettes. Even if she hadn't, there was a good chance Vincent hadn't counted either. Out of sight, out of mind.

But also out of sight, out of mind was what woke her, and the email in her unsent folder, asking Wendy about looking into the 'Brown incident'...maybe instead of the 'Brasco affair'. But the missing tape so distracted her, that it encouraged her to get back to listening to the remaining tapes, and quickly as possible; the idea being to see if she could detect a break in Vincent's narration. He might even go into the 'Brown incident'. Who knew?

He lived in a few New York boroughs, where much of the family still resided, before moving to Philly after his stepfather put all ten of them...him, his four brothers belonging to his father, plus Voge and the four kids they shared...out in the streets. That was a rough period, saved by the fact that he and his brothers were old enough to make real money. Things got interesting, and real fuzzy at this point. He remembered the exact number of stretch-marks on his stepfather's behind after he and his brothers stomped the man's clothes off for hitting their mother—the reason they were put out in the street—but then couldn't recall who he was accused of killing, or why, or how he avoided prosecution.

Remarkably, despite the toasty voice and obvious precision

it took to not incriminate himself, his story was clear-headed and OCD methodical. He definitely had a tooth to pick with his step-father, and took regal time going to extraordinary lengths to floss each tooth detailing the ham-fisted deacon with the giant paws, for the first time seeing his mother speaking in tongues. Many Sundays straight, four children later, the man had been banging that ham bone on podiums, talking about fearing NO MAN, but almost passed out when after he and Voge had gotten into a bedroom tiff, she doubled him over at the groin using solely the power of her chant. That was the first time an ambulance came for him. He was diagnosed with a testicular infection, likely from his habit of one too many "spiritual" holidays to homes for not exactly anointing purposes. Vincent's narrations were 100% straight-forward and colorful, until it was his turn to spin the arrow around. Wendy was going to notice, and demand the craters be explored, unless however, she did something to cover them up.

Except, why would she want to plug these craters? She wasn't supposed to be on his side, even if she found herself invested in his story. Overall, the narration checked all the boxes. He and his brothers were hilarious, and of course the murder of his father and the family's struggles raw and touching. She didn't care for his big breathy, likely alcohol-induced speeches though, especially his proclamations on women. She was on the verge of throwing the entire project in the toilet when in the library he got to talking about men writing better than women. Just look up misogynist and there'd he be, a hand drawn picture of him...tail, feathers, and a sling-shot made from animal parts.

A hand full of Tylenol, extra-strength, helped get through listening to the immense pleasure he took elaborating on the seeds he spread across the country...and globe. 'His pattern' of peppering the world with hundreds of children ranging from white-white, to midnight black, speaking 20 different languages was not fun. No matter how much sugar he used coating how he fed, clothed and housed these little people, he was getting a beating in ratings when half his audience... namely people siding with professors like the one at Duke... found their jewels in knots learning how he treated the mothers who didn't want anything to do with him. He made it abundantly clear, using four and a half tapes, front and back, the equivalent of four and a half hours of nonstop rant, on what he would do about any woman who tried to hem him up with the American bureaucrats over child support. Scary. No wonder why Michelle had no reason to leave her boo. She couldn't make much money with her dead, or him in jail.

Fact was, he was brought up Catholic, though worshipped

no religion. He just believed, and vehemently so, women created an inharmonious and imbalance in societies when they wanted to take on roles suited for men. At one point, and she laughed out loud, almost choking on a grape she'd been popping one after the other, when he switched gears talking about, "wanna get freaky, come to America! Wanna meet robots, come to America! Wanna be bossed by two titties, come to America!"

This guy's book was going to kill it. Maddening as the tirades, her eyes and ears stayed so wide open she could back in a fleet of semis. "Sex ain't nasty and love should never go out of style," was one quote that resonated, and not because it sounded warm and fuzzy, but because he backed it up with science he read, comparing mating similarities between animals and humans being tied to natural (unwritten) gender laws governing species.

"Life works like a see-saw," he contended. 'If everybody jumps on one end, game over!'"

By the final tape though, her feet couldn't feel the floor, and her head felt as if he stuffed it with cotton balls. For a reason she wouldn't be able to explain until much, much later, she ran around her apartment in search of mailing envelopes and tape. It became critically important to get rid of those tapes, and she focused on nothing else but ensuring the tapes were securely sent, certified, directly back to Vincent.

Later, the same evening after air-hockeying the tapes to the other side of Fairmount Park, Wendy called. "What is this you sent me," she asked.

"Oh, that's a rough draft of the tapes I transcribed from the Brasco project," she casually replied.

"—Wait! What?" Wendy shrieked. "What tapes!?!"

"Well, he recorded his story—"

"—He recorded his story?" Wendy echoed as if she said she'd taken a picture of his voice.

"Yes, he didn't want to be taped, and the library is only open several hours a day, the majority of them when he's working."

Actually, the transcript she sent more than covered the summary of topics Wendy wanted addressed. That was 17 hours of transcript, compared to the 20 bullet points she threw together.

Wendy didn't hit her back with anything right away. She was busy digesting the snarky quip Rachel clipped on the end of her sentence.

"...Ugh...I still need you to come into my office," she said when her inner turmoil straightened out. "And bring those tapes!"

Rachel was quick that time, catching her before the click! "I already mailed them back," she blurted, squeezing her eyes shut.

A guttural silence followed. Apparently, as Rachel realized after reading the summary, Wendy wanted Vincent to elaborate on a 10-year-old unsolved case, about an incident that occurred five years before Michelle met Vincent, when he and his brothers, and cousins worked on a home where a girl went missing.

"Well...you need to call them and get them to give back the tapes," she instructed, as if she was Lord over cassette tapes.

"No problem," Rachel replied, despite there being a huge problem. Vincent's radar would sound like a 10-alarm fire. There was no way she could tell him 'the dog ate the homework' just to get back the tapes. She wouldn't dare.

"...But Wendy," she eased out, just quick enough to beat the click. "I made sure everything in the summary was addressed. Would you like for me to send the entire draft?"

This time the guttural silence was deafening. If she were a betting woman, she'd put every cent she had on Wendy never being stopped in her tracks by an entry-level employee. Rachel had only sent 10,000 words of story, carefully pasting small sections of the transcript to match up with the summary. No, there was nothing in there about the missing girl (per say), but Vincent had tied enough nooses to choke a hundred times, a thousand different ways. The way he treated the mothers of his children was enough rope on its on. Obviously Wendy presumed what she received, was all Rachel had.

"Of course," Wendy snapped, back up on her feet. "I don't get why you didn't do that in the first place!"

Click!

A few seconds later Wendy was back on the phone huffing. "I'm still going to need you to come in. We have to talk."

Hurriedly Rachel threw together an outfit suitable for an interview, as well as an exit interview, and an hour after the last click was in her office, with a draft of the complete transcript... over 70K words, in hand.

"Look, you did a good job, but we're still going to need those tapes," Wendy insisted. "We can't help your friend without those tapes."

Push pause please. Rachel wouldn't dare contend she was the fastest thinker. Her IQ was likely somewhere in the very low 100's. A hundred and twenty tops. She was a slow reader, priding herself on solving crossword puzzles where the answers were at the back of the book, upside down. Still, she knew when her strings were being pulled.

"Honestly Wendy," she sighed. "You'll probably have better luck catching up with him in a grave, than either me or Shelly will have asking him for those tapes. That guy is not stupid."

The thing was, the manuscript, as it was, was only in need of a library edit, and maybe a soft rub before going to press. Kim, who also had good reading habits, could back her up on this. She got so involved in the story that Rachel couldn't transcribe fast enough before she'd be calling asking if she finished the next section. It was like a running soap opera between them. His stories needed a warning label and FDA approval, and his storytelling was second to none.

But Wendy had no conscience. Absolutely no conscience whatsoever. She could care less about Michelle, or any woman she supposedly advocated for. She was little more than drug dealers pimping goods, regardless of its addictive, illicit, and unhealthy quality ...so long as there were buyers.

"But we're prepared to fork over a 50K advance," Wendy said. "I don't see how we can do that without those tapes."

See. No conscience. "Well, what was he going to get without the tapes?"

Wendy thought for a second, knowing damn well neither money, nor a contract had ever been discussed. Vincent hadn't mentioned money either. He high-jacked her story likely assuming he would get paid once the story hit the streets. On her end, she was already drawing a salary, with a clause in her employment contract for royalties she would receive on special projects such as this. So, she saw ahead what was likely to happen if Vincent heard someone talking about his book, or saw it on bookshelves in stores or, (all angels on their side), saw this book plastered across billboards. He would hound them to death about getting paid, and he wouldn't be asking for no 50K. He'd be looking for millions.

"You're right," Wendy replied. "We gotta get a contract for this guy."

You think!?! That was Rachel's expression, though the look wasn't easily readable on her face. She also was thinking, whatever the fallout from the (surely) unconscionable contract about to be whipped up, she planned to self-publish the book herself if all went south. Smart as he was, he wouldn't know the difference; so long as the ream of paper had a spine, a glossy cover, and could be held in his hands.

"...Just see what you can do about getting those tapes back, and I'll work on a contract to get this puppy moving," she said, tossing about 2 pounds of fastened paper to the left of her computer screen. The draft landed on a scattering of other paper was a good sign, considering where it could have landed. In the trash, which at 11AM was about ready for a dump.

Slouched down in her seat, with her chin buried in her coat, hat pulled down to the bridge of her nose and huge dark BeeGees sunglasses covering her eyes when it was much too warm for the attire, well into the autumn of April, the last hill of snow in the parking lot melted and gone, she met Kim in their favorite mom & pop spot. This was the place where state reps, senators, governors and engaged citizens often convened to hash over community issues and receive generous updates. Kim was an engaged citizen, so meeting here was her suggestion. It also was a halfway location between her job in King of Prussia, and Rachel's apartment in Conshohocken.

She laughed out loud soon as she saw her sister. "Would you take that hat and them glasses off," she playfully huffed. "You look ridiculous...like you're begging to be knocked over the head and mugged for your earmuffs!"

"It's not funny," Rachel scoffed. "I think Wendy's going to put the mob on me if I don't do what she wants...and that guy is going to kill one of us if I do!"

"Oh, stop it," Kim chuckled rolling her eyes. "The mob phased out with the Klan and the Temptations," she laughed.

Rachel had to laugh too. She probably did have too much internet in her. Okay, so slap her with a back-hand algorithm. And still, the contract Wendy drafted and wanted delivered to Vincent, and signed by him, could get someone very hurt. She could end up spending the eternal part of her life in an itty-bitty urn on top of her sister's mantle.

"I just don't get why some people are so freakin' mean and calloused, and then try to hide behind their frail little shero capes," Rachel pouted.

"I don't know either," Kim quipped. "Have you tried asking yourself?"

Rachel twitched up her face. "I'm not trying to be a shero, and I'm not calloused!"

"But you used to look up to them," Kim replied. "I still remember you coming to me all lit up about going to work for Voices. It was all you talked about...those smart, sharp dressed women. Didn't you max out your credit card trying to dress like them?"

Okay, so her sister had a memory like an elephant. That did happen. And it happened again when she was hired fulltime. Now she wished she had kept the receipts. She would return everything. The Wendy and Regina she read about and admired with their arms folded across their torsos on front spreads of magazines, were fantasies. They didn't care about women and communities, and influencing young women to do good in the world. Those women never existed. The Regina and Wendy she was getting to know only cared about their images, mostly photoshopped photos of deeply flawed individuals. It was mind blowing what she learned about them in the weeks she worked on Vincent's book.

Regina married a truly abusive man. Actually a prominent executive not only verbally whipping her, but punching her with closed fists directly in the face. One day she pulled up on the parking lot, rushing to meet with Wendy for one of her 'I need to see you in my office asap' meetings, when she saw a car just a rocking. At first she thought someone had pulled on the lot and was getting it on, right in front of the office building in one of the reserved spots where Regina and Wendy normally parked. Because she didn't plan to be long she parked in a visitor spot, directly in front of a reserved space, giving her a straight line of view. But the tinted windows made it hard to see inside the car, until she saw a white fist wailing away at the passenger who looked like Regina.

Quickly she hopped out of her car and opened her back door to fish around in her workbag. She hoped the guy would see her and stop hitting who appeared to be Regina. It worked. A few seconds later, after closing her back door, the movement in the car stopped. She walked by, and pretending as if it was the first time she realized people were inside, she waved, smiling like she would at anyone parked in a reserved spot. Regina barely looked over though. Her face was buried in her hands. But the guy did look, and meekly waved. It was her husband! The president of KYS-TV. She recognized his chisel square jawline, and much too narrow eyes for his big block face. The pompous dude many called an asshole, who walked around with his chest stuck out a few feet ahead of him, much too important to look down and speak to those beneath him.

Back to the assault she witnessed, she promptly pushed the image to the rear of her priorities, rushing into the bathroom for a pit stop before her ASAP conference. Media moguls didn't accept pacing around lobbies waiting to report possible assaults as an excuse for being late to an ASAP impromptu meeting. And they definitely wouldn't appreciate a pissy wet employee soiling one of their chairs. It would be better to mention the incident to Wendy and let her decide whether she wanted to interrupt her schedule to handle a problem outside her jurisdiction.

As she was leaving the bathroom she bumped into Regina holding a full-length mink over one arm and a blood-soaked tissue up to her mouth. Instinctively she gasped, "oh my goodness!"

"I'm okay," Regina replied. "I just got mugged. But no need to call the police," she quickly inserted in a raspy voice. "I already called them."

Not knowing what to say she left Regina in the restroom to privately nurse her wounds. It didn't look like she was going to have a problem fixing her hair, but weeks later she was still rocking tinted glasses in public and Rachel was fairly sure she never got the blood out of the pink cashmere sweater she wore. The troubling part was when she mentioned the super dark rings around Regina's eyes to Wendy. "Girl, that man is trying to take everything she's worked for," she sighed shaking her head. "I told her she might as well take her chances and divorce him, since he's probably going to wind up killing her anyway."

This may have sounded like cathartic counsel from a caring cousin, but Wendy only wanted to get rid of a headache so she could gain control of Brand Voices. "I tried to warn her when she first started falling for his dinners, ski lifts and private villas," she said adding, "...she walked into that one ass backwards."

HOPE came right to mind for Rachel. First thing she learned was how to listen and dial her emotions down. It was hard because it was easier to trust what she saw and heard around her. Women were not punching bags, and anyone who struggled to see this were as bad as the abuser. But it took women like the Nina's and Michelle's and Regina's to understand women were also not one size fits all best-case scenarios. And the same applied to men.

Like Vincent, everyone came with a story, to include the chisel jawed executive. It served no one justice rushing to judgment. Here Regina and Wendy were supposed to be leaders inspiring women to greatness, but yet were fighting the same basic demons as the young women she met at HOPE. Truth exposed, the women she found most amazing dressed in slacks bought off Walmart racks, and styled their hair in neat natural curls, and wore off brand shoes and sneakers, and rarely any make-up, had plain nails, driving lemons bought off used car lots, and never appeared on the cover of magazines; women who in fact worked at HOPE, and women like her sister.

"Sis, I just want to thank you for going through all this with me," Rachel told her sister who passed on a Walk she planned to participate in for Good Friday, to instead sit on her buns in a clammy cafeteria listening to her whine about more work issues. "I think about all that crappy stuff I used to say to you and feel so ashamed," she said.

"Well, I want you to know how proud I am for the thinking woman you are becoming," Kim smiled.

"Yeah, well...I'd be up a creek if I didn't have you in my corner. Now I'm thinking about becoming a florist... or a Walmart greeter. Anything that doesn't require thinking," she sulked rubbing a finger at a time.

"Whooa...now where is this coming from," Kim laughed. "You are so dramatic."

Rachel was coming from Wendy's office, with a ballsy contract, a cheap check and an audacious demand to personally give Vincent. "Just tell me how does fifty-thousand turn into 500 bucks, and just who does she think she is to demand someone turn over their property... without a badge and a gun!"

Kim laughed. She'd already heard about the whole book deal, in dribbles and drabs. "Sis, just give him the contract and the check. I'm sure he'll appreciate it."

"Yeah, but Wendy wants those tapes. I just know she's in cahoots with a DA. They're trying to set him up...I know it...I can feel it! She's trying to save that damn comp—"

"—Rache, Rache," she said in a hushing tone. "That dude is smart. I read that book. So, forget about those tapes. Just give him the contract and check...and maybe if you just want to feel all toasty and roasty inside, tell him how excited everyone is about publishing the book."

It was a fact. Growing up Michelle wasn't the brightest bulb. Despite what Julia tried to overlook, her child struggled through school. But hard as it was to accept, much less admit, she was one of Shelly's enablers too.

Like Julia writing bleeding-heart letters in her beautiful penmanship to get Shelly into top schools, she helped her pass tests and spot quizzes too, and joined right in with the wild antics they liked to pull; like making a big deal out of sneaking into R-rated movies, running over her mother's flowers, tracking dirt over her floors, and the worst, having awful discussions about killing Julia. For this reason Rachel was saddled with a guilt about the whole Shelly situation, why she was reluctant to totally dog out her friend, and probably what made it so difficult to face Julia.

And even so, last thing Rachel wanted to do was meet with a person beyond help. Actually, Michelle had to see a problem with where she was, which made it preemptive to assume she needed help. And yet, wherever she saw herself, Rachel honestly found it hard to so much as look at her. Sad, but those were facts.

Between Vincent and Michelle, they had been calling a lot. Michelle mostly. She had become her handful's little message collector. 'Did you get Vin's message?' 'Vin said this...Vin said that...' but conveniently didn't read replies. Once Rachel received 50-something messages, back-to-back, sent a minute apart, from Michelle saying the same thing, 'Will you please answer Vin's email! He needs to know if y'all removed voodoo from the book!' It was hard to tell which was worse. No reply or unreadable replies.

And now there she was, with her fingers tightly crossed, trying to arrange a time and place to make sure Vincent got this thick envelope Wendy prepared. Inside was the final version of his manuscript, plus a contract that needed to be read, signed and returned, in exchange for a $500 lousy check... definitely no chat she cared to exchange via email.

"Hey Shelly, how are you? I was calling to see if we could meet–"

"–Oh girl, I'm in bed," she said soon as she heard that one word, meet. "The doctor got me on bed rest for three months. I can't lose this baby. Vin'll have a fit!"

Already exhausted Rachel was in no mood to hear this. Nothing against babies, or women carrying them...or better...the handful's creating them, but seriously. Vincent spreading his seed couldn't be in the planet's best interest. And Michelle being one of his vessels, couldn't be more helpful. But this wasn't her business, and had nothing to do with why she was calling.

Come to think of it, Vincent didn't deserve more than the 500 bucks he was getting. That 49K and chump change belonged to her, for putting together his masterpiece and answering calls and emails around the clock, and now dealing with this bun in the oven.

It took less than 45 minutes getting to their home, which included a stop at Wawa to pick up a bag of Swiss Mix for her, and an Almond Joy for Michelle. She didn't know if she still liked the candy bar but it made sense that Vincent might enjoy reading the contract that much more with his wife behind him yammering about how thoughtful she'd been.

She pulled up and parked in one of three 'unmarked' but coveted spots in front of the house. Given her rapidly sinking energy, and annoyance with the overall handling of the project, even if she had known about the parking situation, she would've double parked beside the vacant spot, than parked a football field out of sight. She just had no energy left for entertaining another hell.

In a few steps she landed on the porch and was about to open the storm door and knock when a guy suddenly burst out of the house next door. He hopped the banister that separated the porches and without using a key, or acknowledging her, opened the door and went inside.

Okey-doke, Rachel thought, making an expression a suburbanite might make, shirking her eyes and pursing her lips into a pleasant curl before knocking on the door left ajar. No sense in getting mauled by a four-legged, or a two-legged mammal when she could just wait for a proper invite.

The same guy who hopped the banister came to the door. He just stood there and looked at her, not saying a word.

"Is Michelle home? Can you let her know Rocky is here to see her..."

He disappeared…and never returned.

'Great,' she huffed, pushing the door open a little more and sticking her head inside to yell at the stairs. "Shelly! I'm here! It's Rocky!!!"

"I'm upstairs," Michelle yelled back down. "It's okay! Come on up!"

She tipped inside and peeked around, using her eyes only. She didn't see the guy that disappeared, but did see a major transformation from what she remembered of the house. It. Was. Stunning. The wood floors wood, shining like glass, and ceiling that belonged in a museum, and the sofa! That sofa, at least 10-feet long, white and uncovered was shaped identical to the one she distinctly recalled seeing Alexis Colby kicked back on. Her and Michelle loved Dynasty! They had the whole collection. That house belonged nowhere in the dilapidated hood she was standing in. That house, in fact, did not belong in the universe! It was out of the world that fabulous!

She found Michelle, feet up and resting on a mountain of pillows, laid back against another mountain of pillows on a king size canopied bed…white and wood everywhere.

"Must be nice," she teased, running her eyes up and down the white walls and over the Cinderella ceiling and bedding. That was an interesting observation however. What man that looked like the handful she'd been dealing with, would sleep on fairy-tale bedding? She could only assume they weren't sleeping together…at least not like normal wife and husband.

"What!?!" Michelle shrieked. "I'm miserable as fuck in this house! I can't leave this damn bed for two whole more months!"

Rachel looked over at her portable bathroom beside the bed. She didn't notice it when she walked in, with all the grandeur hogging attention, but saw it when Michelle flung a roll of toilet paper at the chair. Ouch. On second thought, maybe laying on mills wasn't all it was cracked up to be.

"I bought you something," Rachel said, tossing the Almond Joy on the bed.

"Oh My GOD," Michelle screamed, grabbing the candy bar and holding it up. "You remembered," she squealed, before her face suddenly dropped.

Rachel looked, wondering what was wrong, before following Michelle's gaunt look to the figure at the door. It was the banister hopper. He was standing there just staring. In his hand down by his side was a small dark object.

"It's alright, Gil," Michelle said, waiting for him to leave before she continued talking.

"That's my stepson," she explained, her voice low…and sad. "He's got some issues," she said quietly chuckling while rubbing her stomach. "That's why I'm in here hanging upside down."

As updated and embellished as the room appeared, the atmosphere was an unhappy one. It almost looked like a prison for a spoiled brat, not that Rachel had been inside a prison for the lowest rat. It just looked like a heavy-set chocolate barbie buried in Medieval gloom guarded by a Coliseum monk. She couldn't tell if Michelle was rubbing baby fat or belly fat, or was carrying high or low, or had ever left the house or never left the house. There was no way to either dress it up or down. She took a good look at Michelle and saw beyond the long hallway in her eyes the same girl who used to be called stuck up. Now she was just stuck.

"Vin gettin' on my last nerve with that damn book," she blurted, nothing Rachel said to incite the seepage. "He 'round here tellin' everybody 'bout that book! …Got people around here thinkin' they about to see a damn movie or something! These fools don't read!"

Wow! Just wow. This was coming from someone who didn't read either. "Well, I'm just dropping off the final draft and a contract for him to sign," she said, pulling the thick envelope out of her bag and laying it on the bed. "There also is a check in here, so make sure he gets it."

"A check," Michelle asked surprised. "How much is it?"

"Five hundred," she replied.

"You mean like five-hundred thousand," Michelle asked with attitude.

"No, five hundred dollars," Rachel said.

"That's it," she shrieked. "I bought a—"

"—Shelly, it's just the advance," she interrupted. "He's going to receive royalties for the rest of his life," she explained. Funny though, the book still didn't have a title, something no one addressed. It was all about money and tapes…and oh…making sure voodoo was not in the text. But by this point Rachel was so over the book, good as it was, that she hoped she was in the middle of her third life by the time they realized royalties was a filler that rarely filled the average gas tank. So, she left Michelle waddling in her homemade bliss knowing she didn't have a clue what had been said to her, and got out of there before it was her turn to puke.

She felt good. She left Kim a voicemail: "Thanks Sis! I Sooo So So Love You!"

Then she sent Wendy an email: 'Contract and check delivered! No tapes. Lost them.'

'Great,' Wendy replied...typical of her. She rarely typed more than one or two words. Any response that demanded more thought...and the possibility of breaking one of her fingernails, got her signature 'we need to meet ASAP' response.

But a couple of weeks passed with nothing from Wendy, or the darling duo. No news had to spell good news...a phrase that kind of rhymed with, 'don't start nothing, won't be nothing.'

So she surfed the assignment database from the comfort of her apartment, sipping coffee and getting the googly eyes. Reminded her of selecting college courses. There were countless writing opportunities, each sounding more intriguing than the one preceding it. Hardest part of the selection process was considering who managed the assignment. She'd rather work with anyone but Wendy, and definitely not Angie!

That's when she came across 'Book Fair'...and the name 'Professor Ollie Mustapha-Nweke' listed as project manager. She fell for the job announcement, immediately... before reading what the job entailed. She checked the box beside the heading and continued searching and reading other assignments with far more scrutiny. Until she heard back from Wendy, and was released from the 'Brasco' assignment, incidentally not in the database, she couldn't move on to other projects.

All morning she'd been entertaining the soft hum of her laptop, a quiet if she thought about it, she hadn't heard in a while. No dogs barking. No birds on the windowsill chirping. No car doors slamming or car engines running or horns blaring or sirens screaming. No noise whatsoever. Usually she'd get a call, if not from Wendy asking if she heard anything from Vincent, then it would be her sister checking in, or a telemarketer call she always let go to voicemail. She'd gotten quite a few emails from Mustapha-Nweke too, sending megs of literature on South Africa, along with spammers trying to lure her to click on their trope-crashing links.

She opened Vincent's email immediately, and immediately her heart dropped. The screen, top to bottom, was filled with characters. At a glance it looked like Russian, or Greek text. The alphabet looked rearranged in every possible combination. What begin with 'gnp det n trills' ended with 'kin kiss my ass!'

She sat there staring at the message wondering if he wanted this passage inserted somewhere in the book. It was highly unlikely, but a far better wonder than thinking the book deal was off. That would be, GASP, the worst because then he might not let her self-publish it, which was a deal always on the table. But then too, he could've been testing her IQ, sending her a cryptogram teaser. It wasn't until she carefully scrolled over each line that she got the overall gist of the message. Deciding on her own understanding of the English language, placing punctuation where it needed to go, and eyeball-correcting the spelling, he was pissed about the contract. And why wouldn't he be?

She had read Vincent's (ballsy) contract, and compared it to a standard book contract kept in the database. The two shared few similarities beyond the 'general matter', though granted, contracts were modified all the time depending on the book. Even so, she couldn't think of a single, solitary reason Wendy would insert CLAUSES that listed crimes Vincent supposedly committed, where the families, witnesses and 'living' victims themselves could not only personally hold him liable, but that the publisher, or editors, alas Wendy herself...and Rachel notwithstanding, COULD insert any crime he either discussed with them, or gave them permission to transcribe from tapes he submitted. WTF!

Some nerve! Some astounding audacity. First of all, what right did either of them (her or Wendy) have to willy-nilly-chilly insert dialogue in his story and then ascribe personal liability to him when he DID NOT contribute those stories, particularly that one story Wendy, herself and alone, took great pains to describe in HER WORDS. Again, the contract was all kinds of ballsy, though most astounding was despite his limited writing abilities, he not only could read, but actually did read the entire contract, and called her on it. Literally.

Her phone rang seconds after deciphering his email.

"Hey, you get my email?"

"Umm…yes, I just got it," she replied.

"'Dat woman wasn't no girl! 'Dat was a grown ass woman! 'Dey questioned my brotha' for two days 'bout 'dat ho'," he argued as if she was Wendy. "'Da state tryna' to pull some Scotttsboro Emmett Till bullshit… 'dey betta' get outta here wif' all 'dat!"

"Seriously," Rachel obligatorily sighed. What got her was Vincent's referring to 'they', as if more than Wendy chose to author her (or his) personal point of view and insert that matter IN HIS CONTRACT. Also damning, was how Wendy so obviously, and and oh so wrongly misjudged Vincent. She thought he wouldn't, because he couldn't, read the contract. Ha Ha. News for her. He could and he did.

"Who tryna' put 'dat shit in my book!?!" he lamented.

"I'm sure it's a marketing angle," she replied, the quickest explanation she could come up with on a fly. Really, from her view, and limited publishing experience, if Wendy slipped that gossip in the book, she could end up the defendant, not him. It was why she turned the page when she saw it in the contract, which got beneath her skin too. Just not as deeply as it touched a nerve in Vincent.

"Look, I gotta go up to New York 'dis weekend. My grandmutha' needs some work done in her kitchen," he explained. "How 'bout you ride up there with me so we can talk about 'dis?"

GULP. "Well, let me talk with my boss," she coolly replied, thinking faster than she ever thought before. "We're supposed to be putting the finishing touches on your book this weekend," she added. "You know we want to see this book on shelves before fall."

"Naw…I didn't know 'dat," he said. "Ump…that soon huh?" Sounded like he was thinking too, though taking his time. "Well, call me back afta' you talk to your boss. I got some more stuff I need to talk to you about."

After she hit 'end call', she tapped Kim's number right away. "Okay. I'm really serious this time. I'm dead in the water," she blurted into the phone.

"What happened," Kim asked part amused, part alarmed.

"I just got off the phone with family man. Now he wants me to go to New York with him!"

"Aww Sis, come on," Kim sighed. Sounded like she was getting bored with the up and down, back and forth, hot and cold, I'm about to drop out, no I'm not drama. Shit or get off the pot she seemed to be saying. "This whole thing is going to end in one or two ways…either really good, or really bad. Balls in your court!"

That was a visual hard to look at, but an easy choice.

26...

Without checking with Wendy, she pulled up the biggest pair of panties made and met him at the airport. No, they weren't flying. This was just a convenient halfway point to meet and leave her car.

"Girl, 'dis ain't no overnight trip," he laughed. "What all you got in 'dat bag!?!"

"Oh, I don't roll like that," she teased, relieved he had dialed down the anger. "Just because my girl ghosted me, don't mean I'll do her dirty!"

He burst out laughing, as she knew he would. He liked to keep it real, and had an intuitive sense few could match. Street smart was one thing. A bloodhound was something else. "Na, I'ma happily married man," he chuckled. "I don't roll like that either."

Before her seatbelt clicked however, he was all business. "So, who's actually publishing my book?"

Even for the smartest man (or woman), Voices' publishing set-up was as convoluted as its overall operations. The company itself comprised of four major divisions; Radio, TV, Internet and Print. Each of the divisions either had its own imprint, often a few, or a nexus to one of the big imprints. Cut to the chase, to answer Vincent without appearing like she was trying to be deceitful, the last impression she wanted to give in this situation, she told him Voices was publishing the book. In actuality, she really didn't know. In his contract, still unsigned and not returned, similarly to the fact there still was no title, there as well was no mention of which imprint was putting their stamp on his work. Throughout, the contract referred to "the publisher" as Brand Voices, Inc. "It's a thousand bosses in that place," she lazily added. "...All running around calling themselves the SCC."

He chuckled. "What's 'dat stand for? ...SCC?"

"Sisters coming correct," she chuckled.

He chuckled too, snidely albeit. "Wonder what 'da boys sayin' 'bout 'dat! Any brothas working in 'dat place?"

"Yeah, it's a big company. A lot of men work—"

"—Well 'den, it should be called 'da SBCC," he scoffed, before laughing, "'dat shit sound like a animal shelter!"

"Well, anyway, I ain't never heard of 'dem," he continued. "Is 'dat who you work for?"

"Well," she sighed, and heavily so, "Brand Voices might not be known like CNN...or one of the ABCs, but it's a big group with hundreds of bosses split in four divisions. I happen to, at least for now, work for the vice-president..."

"...Oh, for real," he said, his voice marked up, sounding impressed and surprised. "I thought you might of been one of 'da chicks 'dat typed papers and ran errands."

And there he went, going to the side of him she least liked. "Well... if we really think about this...it's exactly what I do."

The car got quiet. Extra quiet, before he sneered, "so, is 'da vice-president 'da one tryin' to put 'dat bullshit in my book!?!"

"She can't put nothing in your story!" Although Rachel ignored that line in his contract, it pissed her off all over again just thinking about the concept. For Wendy to even think it was okay to take advantage of someone she assumed knew no better, was as bad as how all the women she pretended to care for, got into their situations.

Next thing she knew, 56 miles closer to New York Vincent was talking about how he didn't agree with killing babies. "I wasn't about to let her go in 'dere and see 'dat butcherer!"

Rachel froze, before turning around in the seat, her back against the window so she could face him. "Wow. Shelly was lucky she met you. Not a lot of guys step up for black women." What she really meant was it was fucking obnoxious of him to make that kind of decision for Michelle. But she switched up her verbiage to keep from getting on his bad side. There was more than her life at stake.

"Hey, 'da way I see it, 'deez mutha'fuckas' tryna wipe y'all out. 'Dey built prisons, hospitals and schools to carry out 'dey mission," he spewed. "So y'all can thank me for tryna' save y'all from becoming extinct."

'Great job,' she muttered in her head, exercising her right to remain silent while he continued talking about 'they' and 'them', and bragging on him. He went from saving Michelle, and the life of Teton, who happened to be white and black, to talking about the corruption in New York being the reason he had to help his grandmother.

"'Dey tryna' charge her a mortgage to rebuild her new kitchen..." he argued, speaking of his grandmother. He could rip out a wall, rebuild it, rewire it, and paint it in a week. He was going to save his grandmother 10K less than what 'they' had quoted her.

"'Dey shoulda' came to Philly wif' us," he contended. "'Dey'd have a whole lot more house for a whole lot less money," he further claimed. "But 'dey 'da type 'dat would ratha' cut off 'dey nose to spite 'dey face."

He was speaking about his father's people who didn't get along with his mother. They didn't care for Voge's bad energy, also known as the voodoo she practiced... the 'getti' he didn't want mentioned in his book.

As he preached from his personal soapbox, moving from his peeps to other peeps, she clipped glimpses of his nails again—still filthy, and his swollen knuckles—still calloused, and a large gold ring with an onyx stone and maybe diamond center on a pinky finger. Now, that was new. It looked like a class ring, which since she doubted he finished school, she assumed it was a trinket he received from mastering a class in prison.

To her surprise, Grandmother Zeasy, or Z was not what she expected. She was tall, slim and cultured, something like Mrs. Perkins. She opened the door and ushered them through a modestly decorated living room, and into a dining room where a long table was covered with food.

"Are you hungry?" Grandmother Z asked.

"I'm always hungry," Vincent replied. "Tu fais tout ça pour moi ma'ma?"

"Sabes qué lo hice. Kiyes sa? Yon nouvo?"

"Naw, she's writing a book about me," he replied.

"Acerca de ti," she shrieked, laughing loud. "¿Para qué?"

"Pou fè lemonn konnen ki jan yon bon moun mwen ye."

"No pierdas el tiempo de esta buena chica," Zeasy replied. "How's...umm... what's her name?"

"Che-Che," Vincent spat. "Ella está bien."

"Good," Zeasy quietly sighed. "Sera mejor que la cuides. Ella es una buena chica."

"I know Ma'ma. Voy a cuidarla bien."

"Mas te vale. Tu padre sacrifico su vida por ti," she said.

Whatever was said Vincent became visibly agitated, and after a few bites of finger food and quick inspection of the kitchen was ready to leave. "We gotta get back," he told Zeasy. "But I'm comin' back up here wif' some guys and we'll tear all 'dat out. You got the appliances?"

"Well, yeah," replied Zeasy. "But I did not want to have

them shipped until the work was complete. How long will it take?"

"Well, go ahead and have the appliances shipped so we can hook everything up while we're here. 'Dat way it'll only take about a week. You have some place to stay?"

"Yes I do! Right here," she adamantly replied.

Vincent looked at the woman but didn't reply. He hugged and kissed her on one cheek, and got back in the car sucking his teeth. "If it wasn't for my fatha' I would have nothing to do with 'dem putas," he seethed. "She never liked or trusted us, but don't mind showin' her teeth when she want somethin'! 'Dat's why she don't have no man. Don't no dude wanna put up wif' her shit! See… she part of the conspiracy too!"

Rachel looked out the window. With the towers gone New York looked like a vessel being swallowed by the Atlantic Ocean. Bend over the Statute of Liberty and that place would be gone. The further the skyline moved behind them, the happier she got, and not only because she looked forward to getting back to safer territory. She hungered for silence. Noise had a habit of stealing light. And without light, she couldn't see.

By the time they reached the Pennsylvania border she didn't know whether they were in Juba, Aruba or a Durian that fell out of some child's hand and was rolling along a road in Cuba. Vincent wasn't only a talker. He was a philosopher. Suit and mic' that guy up, she'd put not just all her money on him winning a presidential debate. She'd put her life on him saving the world.

27...

Back in her apartment, seeing at last, with all 8 fingers and two thumbs on her keyboard she edited Vincent's contract, removing the entire CLAUSE section. Satisfied with the document, she pasted the signature he Hancock'd on the other contract, to the properly edited contract and sent it, along with the final version of his story, to Wendy. "Signed" she typed in the subject, and "Done" she typed in the body of the email…along with her initials—ROJ—beneath the one-word message.

As expected she received an instant reply, probably typed while backing out of her parking space telling someone in Jersey she was on her way. "We need to talk!"

Normally she would drop what she was doing and call Wendy immediately, like the scared rabbit she was when the project first began. But shaking and jumping every time she saw a 'W' and high heels got old, in the same way the magic of working 9-to-5 in the studio died. Making hair and nail appointments, plus the whole dry-cleaning exercise, and a cart full of other inconveniences it took to sit in an office 8, 9, 10 hours dealing with a half dozen distractions, plus work, got old very quickly. In the weeks she'd gotten to know the high-level diva, the clearer it became, they both stepped in a pair of panties the same way.

So, she let the phone hum while she flipped through Vincent's manuscript, letting Bonnie Raitt finish her 54-minute 'Luck of the Draw' album. Music often altered her sense of reality. Like when she played Tupac or Arrested Development, no one couldn't tell her she wasn't a tough boss. She had survived working at HOPE. Rode the subs and trolleys. Escaped the bottle Vincent had thrown at her and her sister. Graduated from Penn. Cursed out an executive…and still kept her job. That wasn't hip-hop boss. That was tip-top boss...juice that flowed through her veins every time she cued up the music. She'd get to rocking her neck and tooting her lips as if she made some really bad people feel her thunder. Of course, she only roared like this when she was home alone with the shades and curtains drawn. Pulling off bad in private was fun. Publicly however, she pulled the earbuds out and paid attention.

An hour later she finally picked up the phone when it hummed off the arm rest. "Hello," she said, as if she didn't know who was calling. Wendy's number wasn't only in her contacts. It was at the top of the list among her favorites.

"Who do you think you are to negotiate a contract on your own!?! Do you realize you are playing with fire!?! You can not only lose your job, you can wend up in jail!"

"And so can you," Rachel blurted, her heart thumping like a drum. It took a lot of gumption to spit that line out, and she realized this the moment she did.

The air seeped out of Wendy. Rachel could hear it. There was an unmistakable pause before she spoke again. "How do you figure," she asked, ripping the brows off Rachel the way her mother used to snatch old band-aids off her knees.

"He can read," Rachel replied. "They cannot pin that crime on him because he did not do it, Wendy."

"Wha...how...who..." she stammered, trying to get out a group of thoughts at one time. "That guy is a stone-cold killer," she settled on. "He's conned you. That's what these thugs do... get little naïve girls like you and your friend to fall for their crap. They know the game, Rachel. That's why we have seasoned professional experts to handle these dangerous men—"

"—but if he was guilty, he'd be in jail..."

"...Oh child, you have been so deceived," Wendy sighed, as if she'd been trying to get this point through Rachel's thick skull for hours. "It sometimes takes years to get these people off the street. You watch too much TV."

Rachel's rifle was loaded, unlocked and cocked. She had a lot to say to this point. At the rate Wendy had the so-called experts solving crimes, most of their missing victims had probably died of old age. But she wasn't trying to argue that Vincent wasn't a bad guy, or had done some truly awful things. What she disputed was Wendy killing her spirit, her morale, teaching her that this was the moral and just way to take down people she didn't like or agree with. And it really angered her, seeing her mother in Wendy. No child should have to teach a grown ass woman this.

"Do you realize, by putting that man behind bars will help your friend!?!"

Oh, come on now! Really!?! Playing that beat up violin... "Wendy, she loves that man. He's spending over fifty-thousand dollars for their son's education—"

"—Yeah! Probably of my money," Wendy shot back.

She got quiet, though not because Wendy could've been right. Their argument was just going in the wrong direction. It was not the point. "Well, he's not going to sign that other contract," she finally said...and meekly so. "...Not with that clause in it..."

"And so you decided all on your little naïve own to change it to his liking!?! What else did you change!?!"

She was asking her? Did not she have a copy? Had she not read it? Other than removing the CLAUSE, it was the same contract. But she said none of that. "I just didn't know we could insert whatever we wanted in someone's work," she replied instead.

"Editorial license," Wendy clapped back, sounding as if she was examining the contract with a magnifying glass. "He's still going to jail," she railed on. "The state has his deposition. He lied under oath."

"Well, what did he lie about? Do you have the deposition?" The real question was, what was she doing over in the State's business... way outside her lane.

"Rachel, lying in a deposition is a federal offense! That's basic law. You should know this stuff. He's going down, as well he should!"

Rachel leaned back, away from the phone, as if she could distance herself from a person okay with watching executives punch her cousin in the face, but ready to send a man she did not know from bean dip, and who she hadn't seen do squat, nor threatened her life in any way, shape or form... to prison for the rest of his life. How ironic.

"Sounds like you're happy another family man is going down," Rachel slipped in. Might as well get a lick in, while Wendy had her by the hair, showing her how to fight dirty.

"Family man," Wendy mockingly snapped. "Boy, you have a lot to learn," she said shaking her head and shellacking her eyes over the ceiling, nothing Rachel could see, but felt every lick. "You're going to learn though," she grimly smiled. "Just you wait and see. You will learn!"

"Oh, so you're still going through with the book," Rachel cautiously asked, her heart pounding its hardest yet. By no means was this an act of bravery, or matter of principle. This was walking by blind faith, putting one foot in front of the other, when she saw no other choice.

"Of course I am," Wendy snapped. "We have a contract!"

Now she was shaken. Perhaps she should've used a little more discernment before sending that contract to a vice-president who had been around far more blocks than she. There was no telling what was going on in a peripheral view that belonged to someone who paid both hers and Wendy's salary. She could have been mixed up in who knew what, in the same window she may have missed a material fact about Vincent. She didn't have to look hard to recall many disappointments; her own mother, Michelle, Penn faculty, Wendy and Regina…for crying out loud…along with countless others, like the many women at HOPE, showing themselves one way, before pulling off the mask.

There was only one material difference between strangers (per say), and those who enlisted her trust. Like the Nina's in the world, while they often surprised her, they rarely disappointed her. There was a girl at HOPE, barely 5-foot, with feet so tiny she had to wear children's shoes, who gave her a valuable lesson as well.

Rachel wasn't in the center at the time, but arrived to HOPE in time to find it surrounded by police dressed in bullet proof gear, helmets, and rifles drawn. She was sure someone's husband or boyfriend was inside threatening to kill everyone, plus himself. Come to find out, SWAT had come for the pint size girl who killed her grandmother, and dresser-drawers' full of babies. Before hearing the story though, Rachel thought the heavy police presence coming for a girl barely weighing as much as a case of soda, was ridiculous overkill. Without protest the girl left the center smiling, an expression of someone who's eyes could be pulled out, an eyeball at a time, and cut up in as many pieces as reportedly the girl cut those babies up, and her screams would never kill that smile she walked out of the center wearing; a damning visual of the many wolves dressed in sheep's clothing.

In Vincent's case though, he was the wolf. Nothing good about him stood out. And when he opened his mouth, things only got worse. So then, why in the name of all things copacetic, breathable and sane, would she volunteer to defend a man more than capable of fending for himself.

The thing was, Vincent had signed 'the other' contract. He accepted her explanation and didn't care if every family who'd gotten on his wrong side came after him with all they had. The State could enlist the whole U.S. of A... military, plus Homeland Security to stomp on his mini parade for the stories told in his book. Likewise, he also couldn't care two burnt bills less about what Wendy was up to, and why she was so intent to get him off the streets. He only signed the contract because he trusted Rachel.

And what does she do?

She modified the deal on a hunch, an intuition she started second-guessing. Now she was stuck with that decision because Wendy decided to roll with it. The next morning she woke up to a rather cryptic email from her. There was no subject, and in the body of the email was one word. Approved.

It took clearing her eyes and washing her face to figure out her request to work with Professor Mustapha-Nweke was granted. In her current mood and mindset she didn't know if it was a good or bad thing, though it didn't stop her from reading more about the project and excitedly planning for the new adventure. Like Kim said, 'that whole Vincent situation was either going to end really good, or really bad.' So far, it looked like Vincent's see-saw wasn't moving, either up or down.

The 'Book Fair' project promised to take her away from the see-saw... Vincent, Wendy, the book...all of it. She hopped into a pair of trendy jeans, the kind with almost a whole leg missing that only poor people way back in the generations wore, and matched it up with a $200 sweater she brought from a boutique selling mostly one-offs. Actually, the jeans cost more than the sweater, which together she racked up compliments from book enthusiasts attending Temple's book fair.

It was a rather small book fair, compared to others she'd previously attended, but this conference she wasn't there to buy books and get autographs. She was there to meet Professor Mustapha-Nweke, who stood behind a table full of books and bookmarks. Before she dipped into anyone's budget to purchase airline tickets, she wanted to get a feel for him and the project he posted on their assignment network.

"Hello my friend," he grinned, displaying two rows of huge white stallion type teeth. "I'm so glad to finally meet you," he said, looking like a stately man who read African tales to school-age children.

She smiled and shook his warm, massive hand. "Have you received the literature I sent you? You're going to love it in Af-free-ca," he exclaimed in a big buffalo voice, enunciating each and every syllable in proper British diction.

Again she smiled. She sure had received 'the literature', all one gig worth. "You can either elect to stay for the length of the conference, or a whole month. It 'tis up to you," he stated with a smile that rang no bells.

"Alrighty, cool," she replied, on the fence about how long she wanted to be in Af-free-ca. What she was sure about, was buying a copy of his self-published book, 'Gratuitous Aid'. He said it was about research he was doing on the relationships between Africans and Americans. On its own it didn't sound like an interesting read, until he promised it was going to surprise her. "This is why it's necessary for you to take this trip with us."

'With us' was a group of third year students and others from the Temple community. So far so good. She purchased the book, at a whopping $29.99 for 349 pages of book, and left the conference without staying to hear him speak in one of the lecture halls. She had heard...and seen enough. Wasn't nothing that man was going to say on stage that would cost his family all the gold and ivory tusks they had to sell to get him to America and in Temple.

Back home, in this static euphoric bliss she called Kim to ask if she could store a chest in her garage while she was away. "So long as it's empty," Kim teased, knowing of course it wasn't. Rachel would leave her front door wide open, with her 72" flat screen in plain view and her house keys in the door lock before she would leave her precious writings, which included a hard copy draft of Vincent's manuscript, in an unguarded apartment.

"Now, how long will you be gone," Kim asked.

"Well, I'm thinking about staying a week, but just might stay the entire month," she decided. "I need to clear my head..."

"In Africa!?!" Kim chuckled. "You do plan to return, right?"

"Ha ha ha ha," Rachel sardonically laughed. "I'll be fine. Rest assure, this is a very different African I'll be working with this time...thank you very much!"

Five days before the Africa trip Wendy emailed. 'Please set aside time to meet with me before your trip,' it read.

This was a first in the historical annuals they seemed to be co-authoring. Wendy never typed please in her messages. And she never typed more than one or two words. Rachel could have chosen to ignore the email however, not the wisest decision, even if Wendy wasn't the VP. The bread and butter of all editors at Brand Voices was getting assignments.

So, she called Wendy's guard and got on her calendar, probably a lot quicker than anyone in the company ever had. Turned out to be a brainstorming session to title Vincent's book. 'A Brasco Tale'… 'My Story'… 'Up From Hell'… and 'Tough Guy'…were a few choices they batted around. Neither cared for any of the hooks, though both agreed they were looking for a bold head-butting title.

The meeting wrapped up uneventful, and unresolved. Wendy had to take a call, and Rachel was relieved Ed had an issue greater than naming Vincent's book. At least Wendy hadn't abandoned the project, which was a great way to leave the country. That chapter was done and over. She called Michelle and told her to tell Vincent his book was headed for print, and she would follow up once she returned to the States. Of course, like Michelle, this was too much info for her. Besides wanting to know if the book was going to be added to the Department of Corrections library, she was most upset about Julia having the audacity to threaten to seek full custody of Teton and Ryker.

"Vin is gonna kill me if she tries to do that," she cried. "She knows I'm still on bedrest and can't be running around dealing with this!"

Rachel sighed. Poor Michelle. Unfortunately, she had neither time, nor mental capacity to brainstorm, and felt sucky having to cut her off. "Just keep your feet up and try to relax. It could be worse...having to run around keeping up with three busy kids! ... And oh, don't forget to give Vincent my message!"

It was a rough way to race through a call, and perhaps lousy advice to give a friend except, was Michelle really a friend, or just someone she used to know? She didn't even have time to beat herself up about it. Wasn't like it would be the last time she'd need a shoe horn to pull her foot out of her mouth...like the day she left the meeting with Wendy, and bumped into a woman she had been calling Plain Jane.

"So! How do I get a book deal...and an all-expense paid assignment overseas?"

First thing Rachel did was look down. Plain Jane was the dowdy woman Liz lined her stars up with, which by the way, she hadn't seen Liz in months. She heard about her though. Her book deal fell through. She supposedly was working at FPN, likely why they hadn't run into each other. No one cared to crawl from beneath woodwork to explain why they attempted to stab a peer in the back, then roll her under a bus, and for the final assault, ghost her.

But here was Plain Jane, who every so often she had seen slipping and sliding around in cheap shoes, why she immediately looked down, curious to see which shoe-bridezilla infomercial she had buttoned around her feet.

"Well, I don't know," Rachel playfully teased. "But maybe you can tell me where you find your shoes. I could use a good comfy shoe while touring the Motherland."

"Oh, I got these at the Shoe Mall...channel 299," she leaped right into explaining. "There's no way I'll ever spend a lot of money to walk around in shoes killing my feet," she said as if this point needed clarifying. "That's why people be walking around with them humps in their back. Nope! Won't be me!"

Rachel looked down again. Looked like the shoes could have been made in anyone's kitchen... with a cup of flour, two eggs, a pinch of salt, and baked at 350-degrees for a few hours. Of course Rachel didn't share her thoughts. She still didn't know the woman's real name, given all the time she'd been with Voices neither bothered to introduce themselves. Before Liz took her friendship elsewhere, they used to talk about the woman, and not nicely.

One day, totally out of the blue, much like this day, the woman appeared in front of them, and with her nappy head, Hershey Kiss complexion and buck teeth commenced to sharing a freakish list of traits she found unattractive in men. Why the woman slid in front of them with this unsolicited conversation, beat all mysteries, told and untold.

Plain Jane stood in front of them, looking like every man's last choice, telling them the guy worth her merit had to be tall, well groomed, smelled nice, looked good, made at least six figures, had good credit, excellent health, owned his home, didn't lie or cheat, and had no children, among other attributes it took her and Liz weeks to finally close their mouth. After that, they talked about that woman every time they saw her, or mention of the word 'man' cropped up in their conversation. Plain Jane was the biggest joke in the company, until of course, Liz befriended her.

But Rachel kept their chat professionally light theorizing some people didn't know how to simply say, 'congratulations', and keep it moving.

"Well, guess I'll have to go with what I've got, unless the flight attendants are handing them out on the plane," she teased.

"…But how did you get that assignment," Plain Jane insisted. "I went to Meredith and got my Masters in Psychology, so I don't get how someone barely out of school got that assignment."

Rachel stared the Meredith graduate dead in both of her half-moon eyes. "…Ummm, I didn't get your name," she replied.

"It's Ann," she said as if Rachel owed her a few bucks for the information.

'Close,' Rachel thought anyways, introducing herself as well, to which Ann shrieked, "I know who you are! Just because you worked at HOPE doesn't make you knowledgeable about women's issues, which I've studied my whole life!" She shifted from one clog to the other and stuck out her ostrich neck an inch further to continue lecturing.

"You are way too pedestrian to be speaking for women who have real testimonies about what it's like being taken advantaged of and abused by men. I was raped when I was 10, and let me be first to tell you, in case no one has told you yet, IT IS NO FUN!"

What made Rachel go to a place she never knew existed, she would swear was a cruel conspiracy devised by a person she couldn't see, but it was too late to recall her words. "That's your opinion, because I happened to enjoy having sex with my 6th grade teacher!"

WELL! Ann's half-moon eyeballs popped open and lit up as if she were plugged into an electric socket.

She asked herself 'why' over and over. The remark was spot on, but so unnecessary. She knew how most of the editors at Brand Voices were. They lived and breathed news. They were like piranhas over gossip. It was their sworn mission to entertain the masses, and would amuse this audience with the flimsiest tales, at the drop of a hat, no matter how unverified, and regardless of who it hurt, or irrespective of how many people were rolled beneath busses. It was their chosen profession.

Mr. Hayward was her 6th grade teacher. Really, he was a kid himself when they met. She was 12, almost 13, and he was 25. Oh, she thought he was so cute, and she fantasized about him day and night. His big brown eyes, and the way he cut them when he looked at her. His dark thick brows, and thin moustache, and oh man, his sideburns really turned her on. She watched his back-side too, and Lord Have Mercy, when he turned around!

And then it happened one day. After he dismissed class, he called her back. "Rachel, is everything okay?"

"Yes," she giggled, oozing inside with excitement.

"I think you're not focused, or rather focusing on the wrong things in class," he said.

"Huh?" She truly was stumped. Suddenly his appeal was gone, replaced by a teacher disappointed about her behavior in class. He was so concerned about her behavior that he called her parents, one of the many tapes hidden in her closet. When she heard him on the answering machine talking about how smart she was, but was distracted by the boys and behaving inappropriately, she got angry. If she was a disappointment to him, then he was a greater disappointment to her.

Eventually he was able to reach her parents, though not

before she had intercepted many of his voicemails. Her parents however, didn't come down too hard on her, because they were going through their own issues. As a matter of fact, this happened shortly before her mother's arrest. When she was talking to Michelle about suicide, part of her anxiety was due to what she described in her journal as a failed love life. She had met another guy, also older than, but not as old as Mr. Hayward. Stuart was a tall black guy with acne and braces who worked at the movie theatre. He wasn't nearly as cute and sexy as Mr. Hayward, but he liked her and didn't mind fooling around. That's who fathered the baby she aborted, though she told Michelle it was Mr. Hayward's baby, because that's who she was in love with.

While at Penn she got curious about Mr. Hayward and looked him up. He had moved to Ohio, but was still teaching public school. He also was married and had children. This part she figured out through his white pages profile.

She felt terrible, and hoped Ann had already forgotten the conversation and her loose-lip leak. Deep in her bones though, she knew it wasn't so, proven hours before she was scheduled to depart the States.

Wendy called. "Say, what time do you depart tomorrow?" She swallowed hard. Why she was worked up, when she had every right to claim herself the victim, objectified the gravity of the situation. "Two o'clock," she replied.

"Good. Stop by my office before 10. We need to talk."

She didn't dare ask why. Or ask if the trip was still on. Or if she wanted to talk about Vincent's book. She acted like she regularly got calls like this, when Wendy never called 'to talk', and then hung up before talking. She was very methodical in the way she managed her time. If it wasn't important she would have already said what she needed to say.

That's what she got, a thought that took her back to something Vincent mentioned in his book. He was describing a time when his brothers, with him and his brother just a year older tagging along, went to the market to 'pick up' some flour for Voge. Of course she didn't ask that they all go to the store. She told Serge, his oldest brother who was in his twenties, that they needed flour. They had just gotten to Philly and had no money. They barely had a place to stay, and knew no one. Plus, Fe-Fe wasn't yet walking and Voge was ill. But with this bag of flour she was going to work magic and make something that would stick to everybody's ribs.

So they got to the store and Serge told them to grab a bag and pack it with as much food as they could grab. 'We were some wild hooligans back then,' Vincent described humorously. As instructed they grabbed the bags and went up and down aisles taking everything that looked tasty. Somebody called police. Maybe two or three people, plus whoever was managing the store called on them. Everybody knew what was up.

They were hungry, and there was food. Only one brave guy who looked like he had a little clout with the store, probably a store manager, attempted to stop them. But armed with only a white dress shirt, striped necktie and a little silver name tag was no match for the lugar Luis pulled out, a little toy he brought with him from New York. No one hung around to see where the guy had been hit. They took off, a bag in each hand, filled beyond the top. When they got home Voge took one look at them and screamed she wasn't touching those bags. She hadn't seen a thing, other than celery and loaves of Stroehmann bread, and every pastry Tasty Cake sold, but knew they left the house with less than a dollar between them. She wanted no partnership in the karma they ran through the front door. She'd rather let everybody starve, than feed the family a meal that could be their last. Nope. She wouldn't touch it, swearing someone would choke to death, or die a tragic death. No one died, despite little by little eating some of the food. But a few months later Luis, who was only 16, went to jail for shooting the manager. Twenty-six years later he was still in prison. Voge always contended the reason Luis was still in jail, was because he took away someone's father and husband. "You can't expect good to come of wrong," was a quote she taught the family, and lived by. 'You can always tell when someone is living right,' Vincent summarized. 'It's not what they got on the outside. It's what they got inside. Good people have peace within.'

Rachel was not at peace. She was riddled with anxiety, rubbing her knuckles and wringing her hands as if she were cold. When Professor Mustapha-Nweke called to check in and update her on their travel arrangements, she barely heard a word.

"We will stay with my family," he told her. "Don't worry, it'll be perfectly safe," he added. Not that she recalled any of this at the time either, but his book 'Gratuitous Aid' blew her away. The stories backing up his many accusations that the U.S. government was exploiting Africans through its duplicitous health aid groups, were staggering. She had no concerns about traveling with him. His ethos reminded her of Voge somewhat, and Vincent too. 'Don't start none, won't be none.' In a mental fog she replied, "see you tomorrow."

Before the street lamps turned off she was out of bed and ten minutes later, on 476 without a drop of caffeine in her.

"Can you close the door," Wendy matter-of-factly said. It had been a while since she heard this tone, notwithstanding, there were only a handful of people in the building at the time. Of course none on her floor, unless the security guard was to be counted.

Rachel closed the door and sat down, pretending not to notice Wendy fussing with papers on her desk. "Hope you don't mind me running in here in sweats," she joked, trying to lighten the mood, or rather...test her mood.

Wendy looked up, and over the rim of her bifocals hanging on the bridge of her nose as if she had said, 'hope you don't mind me flapping my wings like a bird.'

"Do you know Ann DeBerry," she asked.

Rachel scrunched up her face before walking her eyes over her forehead and settling on squinting at the ceiling as if looking for a hairline crack. "I'm not sure," she came back with.

"So, you don't remember telling anyone that you liked having sex with your 6th grade teacher?"

"Ugh!!!" she gasped. "What!?!" She might sleep tight on her flight, if the trip in fact was still on, but she wasn't getting any peace until she detangled this damning lie.

"Just so you know, Ann heads up our research department," Wendy coolly said. "She is our top fact-checker," she said with such a straight stony face that it sounded like she said the woman headed up the CIA, FBI and IRS combined, and she could expect a visit from each before the end of the day.

Rachel giggled. Not offensively. But she couldn't help but be amused picturing feet sliding around in channel 299's early morning special.

"You think this is funny," Wendy asked tilting her head at a ten-degree angle.

"Absolutely not," she replied as if highly offended. "I think this is bizarre!"

"Well, what happened?" Wendy asked again. "Ann isn't the type that pulls stories like this out of the sky."

"Wait," Rachel began, her hands raised, but not above Wendy's desk. "I was talking to a woman who I think introduced herself as an Ann. I'm not sure, but if I recall correctly she was asking me about the trip to Africa, and how I got the assignment. Sounded like she was trying to insinuate something...so I'm not sure what I said, but definitely know I didn't go anywhere near anything that bizarre!"

As confident as she felt and sounded, there was no way if Ann was half as good as Wendy contended, she was on the beginning leg of a trip to hell.

Wendy shrugged, taking great pleasure in tormenting her. "Well...this is going to be very interesting," she sang.

"It sure will be," Rachel said shirking her eyes. A knot the size of a watermelon swelled in her throat and caught her by the juggular. "I can't imagine why—"

"—I actually called you in here because I wanted to show you something."

The lump in Rachel's throat grew even larger. She had no room left to swallow.

Wendy turned her desktop screen around and watched as Rachel's eyes opened like a rose. "Oh my God! That is beautiful," she gasped.

It was a photo of Vincent. A professional photo of his profile. He had really cleaned up.

"Yeah, I got one of my guys to take some pictures of him. We're using it for the cover."

"But do we have a title yet?"

"Hmmm..." she hummed. "I think I have something in mind," she chuckled, before throwing another surprise her way. "By the way, do you know anything about staying with Professor Mustapha-Nweke's family?"

"I do," she replied, breathing in a gush of air and exhaling, the first good breath she had taken since sitting down. "He called last night. I'm cool with it. I think—"

"—Well, I hope you think about what you said to Ann, because if I know her, she's going to find that teacher and bring him and the entire school board down, the way reporters brought down the Catholic church!"

Just like that, she opened her mouth and there was the watermelon, and the grip on her jugular.

Wendy leaned forward, forcing Rachel's eyes to widen in proportion to the melon lodged in her throat. "This is a hot topic, my dear! What were you thinking!?!"

She met Mustapha-Nweke, who everyone called Ollie, along with a group of thirteen in all, at the airport. A cursory intro revealed that most were juniors and seniors at Temple, and only planning to be in Africa for the 2-day book festival (plus travel time of course). The two that would be staying with her in Ollie's family's home was another instructor at Temple—Ben Odemar, and Ms. Cook who worked in the English department. All in all the group looked as open-minded and down for the learning adventure as she who departed with butterflies in her stomach. It was the feel-good kind though, despite Wendy's assurance that Plain Jane was on to her. But at least Wendy wished her a good trip and told her to be safe. She looked forward to reading her column about South African books upon her return.

They arrived in the evening on the continent of their beloved Motherland, greeting a deep blue sky and smug temperatures in a decent range. Not too hot, definitely not cold, even though she spotted one person wearing a winter white knit hat with a furry ball on top. Perhaps it was a passenger arriving from Alaska.

Still, the place looked like nothing she imagined. Before she thought dusty red-hot clay crawling with mostly brown to midnight black people. But take away the signage and she could have just as well been in Manhattan or San Francisco or anywhere in the U.S. where enterprise and a motley mix of people speaking more than one or two languages collaborated. For sure, far more white-(looking) people buzzed around than initially expected. She was tickled by Ollie however, so eagerly pointing this out.

"Americans think we have jungles, but see, look, there's not a single jungle," he argued suited up in a plaid jacket a size too small, and a muscle turtleneck gripping a beer gut and a size c-cup.

They split up to slide into sleek midnight black Mercedes waiting for them and rode to the hotel where they checked into a magnificently lit up building from the outside, but reminiscent of a jungle inside. Usually when she walked into hotels, she'd be more inclined to look around... at the columns and pillars perhaps, or up at the ceiling and chandelier lighting, but first thing she did was look down...at wild black and gold accented carpet, before looking around at huge leafy plants.

Next thing she knew, like all be damn, if a man didn't enter the lobby with a loud squawking monkey on his shoulder. "Eeek... eeek..." screeched the creature looking frantically around as if mocking her and other terrified travelers.

It was funny because the plan was to spend a few days in the hotel, checking out on Sunday, where four of them would continue to Ollie's family's home, and the rest return to the states. Well, the group scheduled to leave Sunday, were ready to leave soon as sight and sound of the monkey announced its presence.

"Don't worry...don't worry," Ollie nervously said. "That is typical. It's normal. It's just a pet. It won't harm you."

Well, Kenyatta, and little pale Allison looked like they sorely disagreed. Rachel only laughed, disarming those definitely planning to adhere to their tight itinerary.

After getting settled in their rooms and tip-toeing around the hotel, declining Ollie's invite to check out other festivities being held in the area, they met up for dinner to discuss logistics.

"Look, there's no guarantee any of this stuff is going to happen the way it's printed here," Ollie said holding a brochure listing the schedule of festival events. "We must be flexible," he continued. "In order to cover the entire event we must split up."

Well, they hadn't even left the hotel yet and half the group were sitting around the table practically locked arm-in-arm they were huddled so tight.

"Rachel, how about you lead one group, and me and Ben will lead a group," he suggested.

Ben had been to Africa a few times before. His father was born in Tanzania, and mother in Georgia (the American Georgia). So he, like Ollie who was native of Cape Town, knew a lot more about the lay of the land.

And yet she was cool with taking the lead, despite having never stepped foot outside North America, and despite Ms. Cook, talking nonstop about children and grandchildren, seeming more qualified for a leadership role. But she didn't quibble. The itinerary made sense and didn't read overly complicated.

She did, however, side with some in the group, picking

over the food in search of what appeared identifiable...and edible; rice, corn kettles and beans. Ollie and Ben however, cleaned their plates, while the rest didn't look so hungry. Look, bravery was for heroes who didn't care about returning home in body bags. She, and a few of the others weren't quite there yet, though watching Ollie and Ben chewing like she did on Thanksgiving, she could see herself soon loosening up.

And that's exactly what happened. The following day she, and those in her group... Leslie (Ms. Cook), Gwinette, Gloria, and Kenyatta hopped on a shuttle bus operated by the hotel laughing at a guy who also hopped on the bus with a set of congas strapped to his back. "Oh lawd, first the monkey and now here comes this fool about to show his tail too," Kenyatta teased. She was the comedian among them, and high on African propaganda as she also joked about bringing along scuba gear so she didn't drink the water while taking showers.

"Actually, the water here is probably safer than that Schuylkill slush you've been drinking," Gwinette replied, clearly offended. She was the realist, a practical African Studies student.

But Kenyatta ignored Gwinette, popping her lips as she talked about an uncle who returned home from a missionary trip to Africa with digestive issues. He died three years, and a half dozen rounds of chemo, later. Terrible story, but the gel that congealed them, like Kenyatta's gel pedicure and matching swathes of vibrant cloth she decided to wear that morning. The girl had it worked out in her mind that she would be blending in, when she actually stood out. Maybe had she just left it at the braids and flip-flops no one would have thought much about the Jumanji dashiki contrasting so sharply against crowds dressed more like tourists visiting Disney World. Quite a few even, particularly the younger visitors as most of them were, dressed like they could have backed up the Beastie Boys in their hey days.

Of course they were excited to be in the Motherland. This was the birthland of the ancestors, a place every black American, at one time in their life thought or talked about, but so few actually got to experience. So dialing up the melodrama came with the elation, with the goal being to take back as many rich and vivid stories to their school papers and columns, as each pair of eyes could collect.

It may as well have been a Nirvana concert they had walked into when they entered the pavilion. The energy was gigantic, like a rave of literature fanatics pushing them deeper into the ballroom filled with books. Literally. Books.Were.Everywhere. And so were people who loved reading and collecting them. There was nowhere to turn and not be assaulted by information.

In that instance Rachel felt woefully inadequate, as if she had been lied to her entire life. It was one thing when Vincent told her how naive she, and most Americans were, but another thing to be at a book fair, where she had been dozens of times before, to see how naive she was. She felt so transported. It was as if Disneyland had moved into the Library of Congress. The four of them almost lost their minds running around the auditorium, touching every book with their hands and eyes.

Every few minutes she would grab either Gwinette, or Gloria, or Kenyatta by an arm. "Ooo! You've got to read this..."

And Gwinette, Gloria and Kenyatta took turns tugging her arm. "I'm taking this one back to the hotel with me." That was Gloria, while Gwinette goes, "guuurrl, do you know if there are any restrictions on how many books we can take out the country?"

Ms. Cook, meanwhile, was way across the gallery eating something from a napkin and talking to a towering heavyset dark man looking most out of place. Even from across the room, roughly a football field spread away, she could make out the guy bragging and lying.

"Damn, girlfriend must be desperate," laughed Gloria.

"...Or dumb and desperate both," Gwinette added.

"...Aww, she's just friendly. She's the same way at school. It's hard for a sista'," Kenyatta laughed.

Soon, they lost sight of Leslie, or rather they never looked for her. She was a grown woman. Older than all of them, who were unmarried and childless. There were far more interesting sights. When they weren't busy opening and closing books, and studying synopsis's, they were busy checking out the architecture of the pavilion. The stained plexiglass long windows, and marble walls and floors, and gold-plated railings fit one word Ollie used a lot; majestic. The place looked regal, despite outside, within a squint's view appeared rows of cruddy crumbling stone homes... buildings that as Gloria pointed out, existed in the states too.

"Y'all know there's a North Philly near every center city!"

"This is true," noted the student for life, Gwinette. "Every country has it's good and bad."

"Yeah, but I heard there are bugs out here we have never seen," inserted Rachel.

"And there are some rats that hang out behind Wawa they haven't seen either," Gloria laughed.

"Shoot, wish we could take some of them home with us so they can catch 'em and cook 'em up," Kenyatta chuckled.

"Good Lord," Gwinette sighed. "This is the reason Dr. Mustapha's lectures are standing room only!"

So true. Ollie spent hours at a time confiscating these type souvenirs visitors like them smuggled through customs to share with unwitting family and friends. They meant no harm however, returning to the hotel several hours later falling into each other laughing about silliness.

"I'll catch up with you guys later," Gloria said, carrying an armful of books into a room she shared with Gwinette. Kenyatta slipped into an adjacent room juggling rolled artwork and books too. There was no Leslie, or rather Ms. Cook. They hadn't seen her since she disappeared in the sea of books.

Rachel got in her room relieved she didn't have to share the space with another human being. It had been a long day. All she cared about was kicking off her shoes and hopping on her laptop to jot down her thoughts. Nothing out of the ordinary had happened. She met no rock stars, though she asked for autographs, and in a few instances took photos...just in case. She was only away from the hotel a few hours, but observed some norms in Africa, foreign in America. First, there were rules to driving in America. Motorists just didn't pull out into traffic, cutting people off because they had turned on the ignition and were ready to go. And yet, she had not a negative thought about the spirited shuttle rides!

Ebu, bless his heart was a talker, and the girls kept his motor going. Despite apologizing for what happened to the Africans "that went to America a long time ago" he might've given Ollie a go on a mic. According to him there were problems in the country, not all related to Western interference. Unlike America where gangs operated on more of a nuisance level, gangs in African countries, which weren't so much as gangs, as regimes or tribes congealed by beliefs and ideals, played a whole different turf war. They operated on levels that had the power to dismantle governments.

She would've loved to have Ebu in her room, where it was quiet, and he wasn't being pelted with questions, some genuine, others pure nonsense. She really wished he was able to elaborate more on the West's history with genocide, to compare his view with what she read in Ollie's book, but he kept getting interrupted by Gloria who wanted to know how many wives he had, and Kenyatta asking if he owned any slaves himself.

The ride turned out as enlightening as fun. Ebu, with his Hershey kissed complexion, was warm and engaging. He exuded strength, detected in his heavy azure voice. She laughed when she got to comparing him and Ollie...and Ben. In Ben's case, he was, as Ebu might phrase it, very colonized (alas American). His yellow complexion and perfect American English and mannerisms knocked him completely out of the Congo gene pool. Ollie however, with the round head, wide flat nose and milk chocolate color looked quite Nigerian, despite his claim to Cape Town. (Her opinion only).

On the other hand, Ebu was a deep dark chocolate dream come true. He was tall, lean, muscular and had sharp features; keen smart eyes…arrow nose and just enough lips to keep her staring at his perfect ivory white teeth.

Summarizing the outing two novelties struck her. One was a phrase transporting her back to America. As they exited the van Ebu said, "be safe." And the second. DAMN! Those Africans knew storytelling!

So, while she joked with the girls about silly stuff, she… and actually Ms. Cook, came to the country to observe the culture. It was why they opted to stay a month, not that this was enough time to appreciate the customs and language. South Africa was a large area to cover, and they would only be staying for what amounted to a minute, in Johannesburg. It would take centuries to fully digest what they wanted to share with American populations.

But at least she had a private room and queen size bed to spread her book loot across, and not be interrupted by someone who wanted to turn on the TV, or talk. Armed with a hot cup of coffee she quietly thumbed through a few books she bought, before letting her mind and fingers loose, racing over her keyboard trying to recapture all she had taken in thus far. It totally blew her away seeing so many sleek black Mercedes cabs. That was a visual that paled in comparison to America's fleet of grungy yellow cabs, and unmarked, and often unattractive Uber rides. She thought about the smug saffron smelling air too, comparing the scent to memories visiting Manhattan, which smelled like a dumpster, and Florida, which smelled like alligators.

After 2500 words of note-taking she thought to check email before freshening up for dinner. Ollie said to be flexible with the itinerary, but she didn't want to entrust figuring out what to eat on her own, or with Gwinette and the others who seemed to know less than her. It took a minute…or more like two hours tracking down Ollie to verify 'expense' protocols for accessing the Internet.

She got a fantastic runaround, a peculiar emerging pattern reminding her of Vincent and other male nonnatives she met living in the U.S. They were the biggest know-it-alls. And both had that overbearing big sibling/overly-protective parent style that rubbed up against her own ego. All she wanted to know was if he'd been given an expense budget because, YES, she absolutely was going to charge her data usage to his budget. Likely he figured this out, faster than the wool she tried pulling over his eyes, though within those couple of hours she was connected and looking at a screen full of email, one instantly standing out from the rest.

Vincent had responded to her away message she haphazardly activated after her impromptu meeting with Wendy. ALL CAPS ON, BOLD text and spellcheck entirely off, he accused her of 'taking off' and 'not keeping him updated.' He copied Wendy on the message.

Quickly she replied To All: 'Dude, don't ruin it! I'll call tomorrow! —ROJ'

One curt email sent she showered and joined the group (downstairs) for dinner. There being no guarantees any of them would make it to dinner after such a long day, she was not surprised to not see Leslie (or rather Ms. Cook). But as she slid in a chair and looked from Ollie's tight jaws to twelve long faces seated around the table and no one willing to make eye contact, she knew something was wrong. No, it wasn't funny, but when Ollie started speaking... "as you can see we are all present, minus one..." she almost burst out laughing! The dramatization of that empty chair was just too humorous to ignore.

But she didn't fall into the table and crack it open laughing. She just snickered, what caused Ollie to stop talking and look her way. "I cannot have this," he continued, his voice firm and his pot belly red eyes fixed on her. "You must talk to your group member and let her know this is unacceptable."

She zipped her lips then. She was in his country and not trying to break any unwritten protocols. After all, she had 3 weeks and 5 days remaining. She wasn't trying to spend the adventure looking for possible ancestors who might have mercy on her and let her stay with them for those 3½ weeks. Already she had roped Wendy up in the Brasco book, and had a top shoe info-wearingmercial guru researching a man who had done nothing and gone on about is life.

"You must remember, there are predators out here who'll eat American women like you for breakfast," Ollie angrily hissed.

Wow! Now that sounded extreme. And just when she was busy comparing Jo-burg to any mid-size city in the U.S. with an unattended crime rate. This expulsion of data convinced her to get even quieter. If Ms. Cook didn't turn up, she could end up there alone with him and Ben, who already knew the lay of the land.

Dinner went quickly. No one except Ben and Ollie were THAT hungry. The only conversations were those being held at other tables, and a maître d' over an intercom welcoming diners to their table. The other night there wasn't so much noise...unlike this evening when the intercom and utensils hitting plates, and glasses clinging, along with extra loud guests celebrating their happiness, making the silence at their table that much louder.

On the way upstairs she asked the group; Gwinette, Gloria and Kenyatta if they knew anything about Leslie. Of course they didn't. They too had been in a semi tussle with Professor Mustapha-Nweke over expense codes and using the Internet.

"She's probably out enjoying herself," Gloria muttered. "I thought about hanging out with her too, but I'm not trying to return home looking and croaking like Kermit the Frog."

Kenyatta burst out laughing. "Gurl, you and me both. I–"

"–So you know where she is," Rachel interrupted. "I mean, did she tell you where she was going?"

"I only saw her at the festival staring down the throat of that big African grinning in her face," Kenyatta volunteered.

"Me too, I saw them too," Gloria added.

Actually, all of them had witnessed that much, and hadn't seen hide nor hair of her after that point.

"Look, let's go downstairs and see if we can find out–"

"–Oh no Ms. Law & Order," Gloria cut in. "I have a flight to catch. I'm just thankful the good Lord let my feet touch the soil my ancestors were taken from so many years ago," she said before suddenly bursting out in a heaving cry.

Gwinette wrapped her arms around Gloria and softly began to cry too. Kenyatta joined in, leaving Rachel standing there looking like the half-African stooge...or scrooge. She left them in their feelings, yucking and memorializing the dead ancestors tethered to their spirits, while she turned around to head back to the lobby. She only wanted their company to speak to the concierge. It was where she bumped into Ollie.

"Have you heard anything," she asked.

"Yes, she's with a local businessman," he replied, his jaws still tight. "They know him," he added, speaking of the women at the front desk she was about to ask. "I'm going to speak to her soon as she returns."

Rachel wasn't present for the dressing down, but was in the sleek black Mercedes driving them to Ollie's family's home when the fight broke out. Apparently, while she was packing and waiting for the car Ollie promised was coming three hours ago, Leslie was at the airport trying to change her airline ticket. She pleaded with the ticketing agents, and cried to security, claiming she feared for her life, accusing Ollie of threatening to harm her. When security failed to assist, she found a USO office and begged for help. A few calls were made. A top security agent showed up. Then Professor Mustapha-Nweke arrived, probably what held the car up. A sidebar heated conversation took place. Things got messy, before the professor convinced authorities he would ensure Leslie's safe return to the States. This was what the argument was about in the luxury Mercedes.

"You are a visitor in MY country! How dare you try to ruin me with that bullshit you women pull in America! THIS IS NOT AMERICA! THIS IS MY HOME!"

At this point Leslie began screaming, "I knew it! I knew it! Let me out! Let me out of this got-damn car right now!"

The driver looked in the back seat at the three of them; her, Leslie, and Ben huddled as far away from the flailing Leslie as space permitted.

"Keep going," Ollie ordered, which prompted Leslie to tug on the door. She was unsuccessful because, fortunately for her, she was seated in the middle, and couldn't reach the door lever... primarily due to both Ben and herself doing what they could to stop her. Neither wanted to be dumped on the road and run over by a motorist who had just stuck his (or her) key in the ignition and was ready to roll over anything, or anyone, in front of them.

But what also stopped Leslie was Ollie, constrained somewhat by his ill-fitted suit heard ripping in places. He leaned over the seat and began swinging wildly. Most of his blows missed Leslie curled up in the floorboard, but the overall fiasco created an awkward start to the three-and-a-half weeks they had left on this trip.

Ollie's family was wonderful though. It looked like the entire village had come to greet them, what made their exit from the sedan a curious spectacle. Disheveled Leslie stepped out of the vehicle with her hair standing in feets above her head. Her blouse hung off one shoulder, and not in a fashionable way. Looked like she could've been in a battle with a primitive creature, and somewhat won, primarily for the fact there was no blood or bites.

The speechless expressions on hers, Ben's and Ollie's face added to the peculiar exit. Leslie's composure was remarkable however. She had enough fortitude not to put on a scene. While the people were friendly and eager to be viewed as normal decent people, it wasn't a far-off guess based on what happened in the cab, that this vibe could have turned 190/360 in an instance.

The first week though was a little rough. Leslie went on a hunger strike, losing a few (necessary) pounds. It took a week before she started opening the door to the room where she had locked herself inside.

"I'm sorry about all of this," she confided to Rachel one afternoon. "This place is absolutely gorgeous, and the family is just intolerably nice."

Rachel smiled. She was so glad to hear it because she did not feel this way about Ollie. During the week while Leslie stayed locked in her room, she sort of stayed locked in her room, only coming out for meals which were off the chain delicious! OMG! His female relatives made an oxtail stew that was to die for! And one of them knew how to cooked collards, better than one of her grandmothers. Few could season greens without hog heels or some kind of pork, but these African women could. The peppers in the greens gave them the perfect kick. She would have asked for the recipe if she thought she could follow it. These women looked like they cooked with their hearts. Every day there was a big to-do over what was cooked, and how the food was prepared and served.

But this wasn't all on the itinerary Ollie prepared. He had a full 3-weeks of activities planned. Visiting famous sites in Cape Town, as in where battles were fought, and national parks where the real kings and queens of the jungle were enclosed...in open habitats and not in cages. They missed seeing Robben Island where Nelson Mandela had been imprisoned and as well missed critical meetings with dignitaries and teachers eager to be interviewed and to interview them. More than a dozen celebrations planned for this visit were dashed. The family realized something was wrong the day they arrived. Of course too, how could this not be noticed with one of them staying locked up in a room refusing food. Ollie and Ben went on to do other things. In fact, they didn't even stay in the house. It was just the two of them, and many female relatives and servants trying to make them as comfortable as possible in the given situation.

But they weren't exactly bored. There was a game room, a movie room and an enclosed pool for their sole use. They also had access to a gorgeous beach within walking distance, and once the relatives hustled them into one of the sleek black limos waiting outside, which took them to a festival held by locals several miles up the coast. This was the evening Leslie broke bread with her.

"I feel bad I kind of messed it up for you," she confessed. "I shouldn't have let my emotions get the best of me like that."

Honestly, though she didn't say it, Leslie had nerves of steel she thought. True, she could have handled herself better, but Ollie was totally out of line. She was glad he didn't stay at the family compound. She might've seen his fat round head and snapped. And yeah, he (or the family) would have gotten her, but not before she got him. She was perfectly satisfied with the trip as it came to be. "Oh, Miss Cook, I think I have enough stories to keep our readers entertained and educated for decades," she chuckled. "...And I can always come back..."

"But that's not the point," Leslie continued. "I should've never let myself go to that level, especially when he was only trying to protect me."

"By beating you!?!" Rachel shrieked aghast. "He had no right to put his hands on you like—"

"—No little sister," Leslie said cutting her off. "It's in their DNA. They are coded and conditioned to protect their women and we are wrong for coming to their country trying to change their ways. I was just thinking of myself, and not how my actions affected everyone else. These people think for the group."

A few days after arriving at Ollie's family's compound, Wendy got a hold of her, asking how things were going. She replied, "things are going well," in her best professional voice. At the time, Leslie was in the early part of her hunger strike and Ollie in an undisclosed location tending to his bruises from a busted trip.

"Well, I saw your response to that guy," Wendy went on. "Good job. I thought we needed to hire bodyguards and take the cost out of his future royalties," she laughed.

"Oh, he'll be alright," Rachel sighed, not amused. She had dealt with Vincent, and now Ollie, and the countless Michelle's and Leslie's dealing with those type men, that the chuckles had been punched out of her. "I don't even think he cares about the money. He just wanted a stage to beat his chest where everybody could hear him roar."

Wendy laughed. "Well, you sound tired. Are you sure you're okay?"

"I'm fine," she kind of snapped, this being in that first week of Leslie's hunger strike. "I just have a little bit of a head-ache," she continued, not entirely untrue. Seeing Ollie throwing those punches at Leslie unnerved her. The sight snatched her out of her body and threw her in the middle of the Congo where she heard the real Africans lived.

"Well, just be careful," Wendy advised. "And do call me if anything comes up. We can always change your airline ticket."

'Great,' she thought. Leslie would've loved to have heard that four days ago. What Wendy didn't tell her however, after hear-ing the drip in her voice, was Ann had caught up with Mr. Hayward. Indeed he lived with his wife and 3 children, in a spacious home in the suburbs of Columbus, Ohio. He was a principal at an inner-city high-school, with a fair reputation.

Several complaints made against him for inappropriately touching children; however nothing solicitous, was expected for faculty working in rough districts. Breaking up fights and wrestling weapons from kids, and restraining them until police showed up was an almost daily activity. This type handling came with the job description.

Yet, this didn't stop Ann from canoodling administrators into believing she wanted to feature the school in Front Page News, using excerpts from students highlighting their favorite teachers. Within days after casually questioning students, gently probing them about times when Mr. Hayward wasn't so nice, she locked on to students least fond of the popular principal.

It didn't take a week before a crescendo of accusations made its way up channels, and the once loved principal promptly suspended pending an investigation. Conveniently, Ann launched the final assault, mentioning Rachel's decade old accusation.

From there the case took off, where the matter was when Wendy called Rachel. The studio was abuzz. Leaks, rumors and accusations flew left and right, all over the country. Though reporters referred to Rachel as the unidentified woman who had been raped by the principal years ago, behind scenes old classmates were found and questioned, to include Michelle who confirmed the allegation. She even told investigators, and innocently so, where Rachel had the abortion. It was the same place where she almost aborted her son. And, as if the unfolding drama needed any more leveraging agents, when Vincent heard about Rachel's abortion, he all but drove agents to the clinic still in operation. In fact, the doctor who was arrested on the spot, had just finished a procedure. He and his assistant were taken into custody, though released the same day.

By the third week of Rachel's stay in Africa, none the wiser, the investigation took a sharp unexpected jack-knife turn. Two individuals were instrumental in making this happen. One was Vincent, who emailed her immediately, an email she wouldn't read until she returned to the States. The other was Mr. Hayward's wife.

Alice Hayward had no affiliation with law, in fact, she was a homemaker, giving her all day long to find out who said what, where and when, almost solving the entire fiasco in one day. Three of the main accusers had long troubling records. Over a hundred parents had petitioned the school, the state, and courts to have that student expelled for his threatening behavior. He was accused of pulling guns on students more than once. Another student was pregnant, for the second time, neither child belonging to Mr. Hayward. The third had a serious case of hepatitis from illegal drug usage.

Not that any of these children's troubles were reasons to

dismiss their accusations, but it was no secret of conflicts between them and the principal. Yet, the contention among faculty, students and none-withstanding, his wife, he was the main voice imploring top administrators to remove menaces from public high-schools.

Alice could care less about the privacy of minors threatening the safety of the majority. Tell that to children so afraid of being bullied, or maimed...be it by knife, gunshot or catching hepatitis, that their parents pulled them from school. The life and liberties of entire communities were at risk. One disruptive child in effect had the power to infect so many, preventing children remaining in the public school system from getting a decent education. Taking down a principal like Mr. Hayward, the main ally fighting for them, was unconscionable.

Oh, Alice Hayward was on fire, though she wasn't only interested in vindicating her husband because she knew he hadn't harmed any child while they were married. She wanted to get to the bottom of this Rachel business. Come hell over high water she was proving either she married a disgusting pedophile, or that damn Ann who supposedly 'accidentally' uncovered this mess owed her an apology.

A search warrant had already been executed on the clinic. The state was looking for records, and or possible DNA belonging to Rachel. But Alice got in the ear of a judge, who issued a search warrant on Rachel's apartment as well. She wanted to see those journals she heard so much talk about.

Rachel was in seventh heaven flying first class back to America, thanks to arrangements Professor Mustapha-Nweke made, upgrading both hers and Leslie's airline tickets, likely they laughed, to make good on his promise and keep them quiet about the assault.

"You should run his butt in anyway," Rachel teased.

"No," Leslie sighed, her voice sounding a little distant. "I'ma ride this one out, all the way to director..."

They both burst out laughing again. Rachel couldn't blame her for feeling that way. She, herself, would never see Ollie through the same eyes again. That man could have another strong opinion and react the same way. His behavior might fly in Africa, but not in America. She turned away from Leslie and fell into a deep sleep. When she awoke, they were over American airspace. She had Wi-Fi access, and so she requested coffee to sip on, while catching up on email.

'Now what', she sighed when she saw Vincent's message; the same ALL CAPS, BOLD font, spellcheck off. He should have been thanking her, maybe meeting her at the airport to kiss her feet, but instead he was up in the air about something having to do with an abortion. She closed out of the email. After Ollie, she just couldn't. There was no way she'd put up with a man, til death did them apart, in this day and age, who demanded she erase so much of herself. What in the freak was the point!

The wheels touched down at Philadelphia International Airport and she wanted to stay seatbelt fastened in, to do it all over again. Not the Ollie beating Leslie part, but the rest of the trip. It was like the time she had Lobster tails. Like collard greens, lobster tails were not easy to cook right. Most were served a little rubbery or tough. But back when she was doing volunteer work, she had lunch at a senior living facility and was served the most delicious lobster she'd ever eaten. Better than lobsters she had at downtown restaurants. That lobster was buttery and tender and a mouth-lounging experience she wanted to repeat, but hadn't come across, mostly fearing there was nothing in the sea that could compare to that meal. A few times she tried, but nope, wasn't the same. Whoever prepared that lobster, he or she deserved three Michelin stars.

But it was time to unbuckle her seatbelt and get back to the daily grind. She really had lots to be grateful for. A good college education. Wonderful teachers and scholars she met, and still had access to. Plus, she had survived Vincent, and cursed out, or at least told off TWO executives and still had her job. And not only that, pulling together Vincent's book was one of her greatest achievements.

Wendy never said as much, but she knew his stories were something like that lobster. Rare to come across. The cover photo for his book proved how pleased Wendy was about the outcome of the project. Knowing Vincent and how wrapped up in himself he was, he was going to love that cover too, what momentarily drew her back to his last message.

What was that all about? She hated to think it, but there was a possibility Michelle lost the baby and that was his howl. That was a whole 'nother bear to tackle, so she switched the channel to avoid thinking about it. Poor Michelle. She would never tell her, but perhaps her boys were better off with her mother, and that baby, if in fact she lost it, was a word from God...and not for her, but for that child. Hopefully Vincent had accidentally, after one too many, laid his elbow on the keyboard. The visual gave her a small chuckle, awaking Leslie who leaned over her shoulder and whispered.

"We survived," she teased. "We made it out of the jungle in one piece!"

"Is that the hook you're using for your column," Rachel teased back. Prior to the hunger strike Leslie was supposed to be covering street dancing. Ollie lined up many festivals to observe and take notes, but she missed the events. She, of all people, next to Ollie of course, should've been laughing least. The columns over at Brand Voices were going to be filled with photos and stories about the book festival.

"No child," Leslie continued teasing anyway, showing no signs of scarring from her ordeal. "I'm writing a cookbook," she laughed as they headed along the corridor leading to the airport. "It's going to be called '100 Ways to Cook Collard Greens!'"

Rachel had her mouth wide open, and eyes closed, laughing out loud. Now that was funny. Ollie's people sure did know how to turn one food product into a ca-zillion dishes, none more so than those collards. She was about to tell Leslie if she needed pictures, to send her a text. She had a folder on her laptop filled with so many images of the dishes his people prepared that she could start a side business selling art for cookbook covers. But when she opened her eyes she met two shiny badges thrust in her face.

"Ma'am, are you Rachel Olivia Jackson?"

Her eyes darted around. Why did he want to know? Of course the stupefied, horrified look told the man he accosted the right dimwit. "Ma'am, please come with us," he bluntly continued.

Too shocked to protest, or ask why she was being escorted to a back office, she followed the plain clothes men trying to guess what she'd done. Maybe she improperly packed her luggage, using a foot to stuff a dozen undeclared books in one suitcase. Or, perhaps someone stuck some contraband in her bags, which curiously, had she the cool to realize it, but Ms. Cook was gone. Nowhere to be found. One badge and poof! The old hussy disappeared. Didn't even hang around to see if she might be needed to hold a bag, or make a call.

"Ma'am, we have orders to take your laptop," said one smooth sexy voice.

"But why," Rachel blurted. Again back to surmising. Did she take an unauthorized photo while in the Motherland?

"Read the warrant," said the same voice, sounding less smooth and unsexy as he handed her a folded piece of paper.

"Wait...wait..." came a shriek behind her. She turned around and it was Wendy, clicking over the linoleum in 4½-inch red boots... top of the designer line for sure, wearing a white wool wrap and leopard fur hat, carrying a huge white leather hobo bag over her shoulder like Santa.

She hustled into the office, smelling not the sweetest around the mouth, holding up a piece of paper and telling the men asking for her laptop that she needed to get work off that laptop first. "I'm Wendy Wooten, president of Brand Voices," she exclaimed, shoving the paper into the chest of one of the men without looking behind. She was busy fumbling over Rachel, stuck frozen to the floor trying to unscramble what was going on. "Let me see the laptop," Wendy huffed, breath tarter than the first whiff she caught, as she unhooked her work bag off her shoulder.

Wendy pulled out the laptop while the men examined the paper she shoved at them. "Where's your power cord," she hurled over her shoulder. "You should always keep a full charge," she advised, against the advice of techs who suggested the opposite. But, oh well. She was more interested to see which file (or files) Wendy was going for.

She plopped the winter white sack on the counter, where an airport agent unrelated to the men, stood watching with as much fascination as Rachel. "This is just going to take a second..." she muttered, breath really kicking as she squinted, zeroing in on finding the file she was after.

The men stood there obediently, arms lowered and crisscrossed, one still holding the piece of paper Wendy handed them. In fact, everyone in the small 5x5 room stood still. Everyone except Wendy Wooten, Brand Voices executive in full on mama bear mode.

Rachel didn't catch what she dragged onto the hard drive she brought with her. It was that quick. She must have blinked and missed it.

"Here!" Wendy said when she was done, thrusting the laptop in the man's chest, the same way she had the piece of paper. "Are we done here?"

The man holding the laptop looked down, while the other one cleared his throat. "I'm afraid not," he said. "We need to check her bag for any other devices...phone...recorder—"

"—Rachel, let them look in the bag and give them your phone," Wendy ordered like supermom.

Stripped naked, robbed of everything she held dear she left the airport, with Wendy...and a flattened purse only holding her wallet, tissues, mints and two ink pens. The men even took her paper notepad. "What the hell was that all about," she asked like someone just given a pap smear by an airport TSA checker.

"Congratulations honey, you've made Front Page News!"

35...

Words couldn't explain, or rather words eventually did explain how truly remorseful she was about the trouble she caused Mr. Hayward and his family. It was the first column she wrote for Front Page News:

New Chief Editor

A Proper Apology.
Rachel O. Jackson

Photo Courtesy of Brand Voices, Inc.

In my case, I grew up in a wonderful home celebrating American holidays with a mother and a father, and two big sisters almost old enough to be my mother. I got the Cabbage Patch dolls at Christmas... frilly pink dresses for Easter... ate hamburgers and hot dogs on the fourth... swam in our family's underground heated swimming pool on Labor Day... attended private schools until 12th grade... graduated, and then gaduated from a top notch college before moving on to work for one of the greatest media groups in the nation...Brand Voices, Incorporated.

Like many, I have a testimony.

(continued on next page)

I've always advocated for women navigating this curvy gender system not always in our favor. Like most things, sometimes we are the victim, other times the villain.

It is not cliché that we all make mistakes. When we take the wrong exit off a highway, that is a mistake. When we give a customer the wrong change, that is a mistake. When we choose a career that is not as fulfilling as we thought it might be, that is a mistake.

But when we tell someone something we know didn't happen and isn't true, even when uttered in confidence, and even if we don't expect to hear the tale repeated again, and that rumor causes someone to lose a job, their marriage, relationships, and a community to lose a valuable resource so many count on, that is a problem.

My greatest mistake, as I see it today, was telling my best friend a secret that was not really a secret, but a lie. We were young, silly, and like kids do, we made stuff up.

Usually, our tales and fantasies stayed between us in our fairyland heads. Like what happens in Vegas, stays in Vegas.

But this secret lie caught up with me and now, though I know it may be of little consolation to those injured by this lie, I nonetheless must apologize to my teacher, to his family and to anyone else who may have been injured as a result of my reckless gossiping.

I can't take those words back, but after working with, and advocating for so many women, it bereaves me greatly to have done anything that misplaced the trust I've built.

No, I can't take back anything I've thoughtlessly blurted, and thought no big deal, but perhaps this might be an appropriate spot to insert an old wise tale I once heard and promptly disregarded... until I learned my lesson.

There was a child who saw a shiny penny on the floor, beneath the leg of a chair. The first time the child went to pick up the penny, the grandfather told the child not to touch it. He didn't say why though. He just told the child not to ever touch that penny.

Thinking it ridiculous, the child did what a child, or perhaps anyone might do, and picked up the penny and stuck it in her pocket. Like what was the big deal? It was just a penny. The following day the grandmother sat in the chair, fell over, broke her back and never recovered. The grandfather looked over at the child and said, "that's why I told you not to touch the penny!"

That old wise tale may read a little thin, but if you think it can't happen to you, let me tell you, it can. Point is, our 'no big deals' sometimes can be someone else's 'big deal'. And it doesn't have to be a sour lesson. Like this woman who was discussing religion with a co-worker. And I know. What the heck, you may be thinking.

But this woman and her co-worker were actually talking about what it meant to be saved. The woman didn't know, and was trying to get the co-worker to explain the event in a logical sequence that even a 2-year-old could understand.

Eventually the co-worker gave up on trying to explain, surprising the woman when she suddenly told her how inspirational she was. The woman, thinking she had made an impression on the co-worker, waited to hear exactly what she said that turned the co-worker's reasoning around.

Turned out, the woman had inspired not only the co-worker, but many others working in the company, to return to night school to get a college degree.

Now, I'm not that old, and thus haven't racked up an immense database of experiences, but have learned how my decisions (good and bad) affect others.

This is not a gender, or class, or color thing. This is a human condition. We all make mistakes. Yet, if there is anything I can do to truly atone for my mistake, it is to be fair in my reporting and storytelling, and never ever again be so careless and reckless in my casual conversations.

When we know better, we must do better.

This is my testimony and my pledge to readers.   ---ROJ

Editorial Blog

MARCH is WOMEN'S HISTORY MONTH

Why It's Easy Clapping For Others ... by RYCJ

Them Joneses.

The fence on the other side with the green(er) looking grass. When you graduate high-school they're wondering what's the hold up with your undergrad degree. And after the undergrad paper, they're flashing Graduate and Masters and PhDs, followed by the car, fine spouse, and children to go with all this.

There are even Joneses living in apartments on second floors talkin' about they (at least) have four windows to throw their pot of YKW out of.

Everyone has something someone else doesn't. No One owns all the letters to success and happiness. HOWEVER, if we stop looking over fences at the Joneses, letting them define what success is and isn't, the greener our own lawn will be. Learn to clap for others' different. The most successful and richest person on the planet is the one who has peace, while alive!

Follow (#oebooks) for more blog articles.

The first call she received was from none other than Vincent. She picked up the phone and heard nothing but yelling. She couldn't tell if he was falling off the side of a mountain, was on fire, or was coming to kill her.

Vincent tried to reach her earlier, when he first saw the poster, but when his book finally arrived, he kept calling until she answered her phone.

"Girl, I owe you," she heard. "Me and my boys was in 'da sub headed to 'da game and somebody looked up and said... "Yo' Vin, is 'dat you!?!'"

"I looked up," he continued, "to see 'dat big ass poster of me! Damn! 'Dat shit was wild. Ain't nobody ever done no'fin' like 'dat for me," he said, sounding like he was crying.

The poster he was speaking of was a 40x60 photo of his book cover. They were posted all over the city...in the subway, on the buses and trolleys, and one was on a billboard, along 76 heading to and from Interstate 95. There was no title. The book didn't need one. His name beneath the image spoke volumes. It was like, if readers did recognize him, all the better. But if readers didn't know this guy, they were going to want to. Worked like a charm, though it was a struggle dealing with the congresses that needed a title in their catalogs. They selected VJC, his initials.

Holding a complimentary copy of his book and crying like a baby...throughout the call... she listened. Never in her life had she heard a grown man sob like that.

"Hey look," he continued after collecting himself. "I liked 'dat article you wrote. 'Dat shit was beautiful," he said, wiping his eyes she imagined. "Yo, look Rock, you gotta come over here and let us feed you."

Other Books *by the* Author

About the Author

RYCJ is a book reviewer, blogger, publisher, and storyteller. Since 2009 she has written dozens of books in a mosiac of genres, and has read and reviewed hundreds of books. She is the ultimate book lover, passionate about reading and writing stories that educates, entertains and inspires.

About the Author